John
&
Abigail
Adams

John & Abigail Adams

An American Love Story

Judith St. George

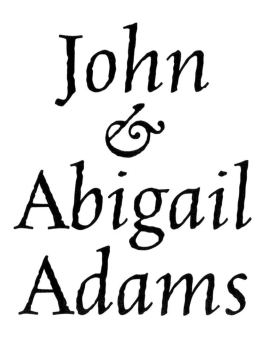

HOLIDAY HOUSE / NEW YORK

Library of Congress Cataloging-in-Publication Data
St. George, Judith
John and Abigail Adams: an American love story /
by Judith St. George.
p. cm.
Includes bibliographical references and index.
ISBN 0-8234-1571-6
1. Adams, John, 1735–1826—Juvenile literature.
2. Adams, Abigail, 1744–1818—Juvenile literature.
3. Presidents—United States—Biography—Juvenile literature.
4. Presidents' spouses—United States—Biography—Juvenile literature.
5. Married people—United States—Biography—Juvenile literature.
[1. Adams, John, 1735–1826. 2. Adams, Abigail, 1744–1818.
3. Presidents. 4. First ladies.] I. Title.

E322 .S78 2001
973.4′4′0922—dc21.
[B]
00-048226

"Love sweetens life."
John Adams

"No earthly happiness can equal that
of being tenderly beloved."
Abigail Adams

CONTENTS

INTRODUCTION

In the past, whenever I thought about John Adams, if I thought about him at all, I pictured a short, stout, prickly, one-term president sandwiched between two giants, George Washington and Thomas Jefferson. In thinking about Abigail Adams, I pictured a strong-willed, opinionated First Lady known to some as Mrs. President.

And then I bought a secondhand book of selected letters that John and Abigail had written to each other. What an eye-opener! John and Abigail Adams were remarkable people in a remarkable marriage, who lived through America's most remarkable time.

After tracking down more of their letters—there were over two thousand—I became a John and Abigail fan forever. They not only wrote about momentous national events, but they also wrote about money matters, problems with their children, illnesses, disappointments, loneliness and such down-to-earth concerns as how to make the best manure heap. Above all else, they expressed an abiding love for each other. (In quoting from their letters, I have taken the liberty of making their creative eighteenth-century spelling, punctuation and grammar more closely resemble today's practices.)

In reading their letters, I also discovered that my opinions about John and Abigail were both right *and* wrong. Yes, John Adams was short, stout and prickly. He was also vain, moody, ambitious and a hypochondriac. On the other hand, he was Mr. Integrity, a brilliant intellectual, a first-rate orator and a born leader, who dedicated his life to his country.

As for Abigail, she was certainly opinionated and strong willed, but she, too, left behind a lasting legacy. One of the nation's best-informed women on public affairs, she helped to shape the political views of her husband and of her son John Quincy, our sixth president. Outspoken, spirited and well read, she championed education for women and advocated that wives have the same legal rights as their husbands. But as an eighteenth-century woman, she believed that a wife's first priority was her home and family.

These two magnetic and extraordinary personalities were equal partners in a fifty-four-year marriage that was unique for its time. From 1774 until 1801 John played a vital role on the national stage. But if Abigail hadn't raised their four children and seen to their education, managed the farm, served as family treasurer and safeguarded their home during wartime, John wouldn't have been free to rise to the political heights that he aspired to.

As partners, spouses and friends, Abigail and John experienced great triumphs as well as devastating setbacks in both their private and public lives. Their love survived years of separation, the deaths of three children, humiliating political defeats and vicious public criticism only to grow in grace and strength. John and Abigail's moving story was a tale I just had to tell.

John
&
Abigail
Adams

Chapter I

Magnet and Steel

When twenty-three-year-old John Adams and fourteen-year-old Abigail Smith first met in 1759, John was not impressed. He acknowledged that Abigail and her older sister, Mary, were "Wits." But he also complained that Abigail, Mary and their younger sister, Betsy, were "not fond, not frank, not candid." As for their father, John noted in his diary that the Reverend William Smith, pastor of the First Church in Weymouth, Massachusetts, was a "crafty, designing Man."

Although Abigail Smith didn't write down what she thought of John, more than likely she wasn't impressed, either. John was rather short and stout, as well as talkative, argumentative and eager to voice his many opinions.

John may not have sought out Abigail and her sisters, but he called often at the Smith parsonage in the company of two friends, Richard Cranch and Abigail's uncle, who had the curious name of Cotton Tufts. John had a keen and scholarly mind, and the Reverend Smith was generous in lending books from his fine library. Furthermore, talk at the parsonage, which covered politics, religion, literature and philosophy, was first-rate.

Abigail and her sisters, who were bright and well read, often joined in the lively conversations. Unlike most young women of their time, they were encouraged to express their views openly—and they did!

Abigail had been born on November 11, 1744. Although a high-spirited child, she was sickly and often confined to bed. There she spent long hours reading and being read to by her grandmother, Elizabeth Quincy. Abigail enjoyed the novels of Samuel Richardson, who wrote about a woman's role and duty as a wife and mother and about the importance of female education. Abigail described Richardson as a "master of the human Heart."

Abigail Smith's childhood home in Weymouth, Massachusetts, was the scene of her first meeting with John Adams.

During the next several years, Abigail viewed marriage only as a remote possibility. She was almost seventeen when she wrote to a friend that there was "a great scarcity of suitors," at least the kind of suitor she might fancy.

John Adams, on the other hand, was a romantic who had always enjoyed kissing, "hustling and gallanting" the girls. "I was of an amorous disposition and very early from ten or eleven Years of Age, was very fond of the Society of Females," he later recalled. John had recently been in love with a beautiful young woman. When she jilted him for another man, John sank into a months-long depression.

Although Abigail found suitors scarce, her sister Mary had found *her* suitor. She and John's friend Richard Cranch had fallen in love. By the time they were married in 1762, Abigail and John had both experienced a change of heart.

Abigail had grown slender and tall, five feet seven inches, nearly John's height. Her fair complexion was set off by her luxuriant brown hair and dark, almost black eyes. John found himself taken by this witty, outspoken young woman. In his diary, he revised his earlier opinion and praised Abigail for being "a Friend . . . prudent, modest, delicate, soft, sensible, obliging, active."

In turn, Abigail saw beyond John's self-important airs and was drawn to his honesty, loyalty, forthright manner and extraordinary intellect. Rather than being disappointed in his plump, balding appearance, she was well pleased that he was no handsome Romeo who might catch the eye of other girls. To add to his appeal, John was not without humor. When he mimicked local Weymouth townspeople, he reduced Abigail and her sisters to fits of laughter.

John's and Abigail's educational experiences were worlds apart. Born

John Adams was the first of his family,
but not the last, to graduate from Harvard College.

on October 30, 1735, John had graduated from Harvard College in 1755 and lived for three years in Worcester, Massachusetts, where he taught school and studied law. In 1758 John was admitted to the practice of law in the British-held Massachusetts Bay Colony.

In contrast, Abigail had never attended a day of school. Only her brother, William, had any formal education. Abigail, Mary and Betsy

Smith had been taught to read, write and do simple arithmetic by their parents and Quincy grandparents. Abigail always regretted her lack of schooling and was embarrassed by her peculiar spelling and punctuation, which she called pointing. And Abigail resented how most families neglected their daughters' education. "Every assistance and advantage . . . is afforded to the Sons," she commented indignantly.

John and Abigail, however, weren't concerned about their differences. To their mutual delight, they discovered that their thinking and interests, as well as their intellectual and political opinions, were very much alike.

But Elizabeth Smith was not pleased to have John as a suitor for her quick-witted and lovely young daughter. She considered John, who lived with his widowed mother and his brother Peter in nearby Braintree, to be stubborn, vain, moody and too ambitious. Mrs. Smith was proud that five generations of her Quincy forefathers had been prominent in the Massachusetts Bay Colony. John's father, who had died in 1761, had been only a farmer, turning shoemaker in the wintertime to support his family. He had held a number of Braintree town offices, but that was of no consequence to Mrs. Smith. Furthermore, John was a lawyer, and lawyers weren't respected or in many instances even to be trusted.

It was certainly true that John was ambitious. "How shall I gain a Reputation!" he had exclaimed in his diary. "How shall I spread an Opinion of myself as a Lawyer of distinguished Genius, Learning and Virtue?"

To gain a reputation, John started his law career by riding the court circuit from one district courthouse to another. Separated frequently, John and Abigail wrote each other long and loving letters. As was the custom, they both took names from mythology. Abigail chose Diana, the Roman goddess of the hunt and the moon, while John took the name

Lysander, the Spartan hero who became the leader of his country after winning a great sea victory.

In an early letter, John addressed Abigail as "Miss Adorable," claiming that she owed him many kisses. "I have good Right to draw upon you for the Kisses as I have given two or three Millions at least."

Although Abigail returned John's affection in kind, she was more reserved. That same year she closed a letter with "Accept this hasty scrawl warm from the Heart of Your Sincere Diana."

Traveling with John on his court circuit in the fall of 1763, Abigail stayed at friends' homes along the way. Soon after they returned, she informed her parents that she and John would marry. By this time Mrs. Smith, who knew what a strong will lay behind her daughter's modest demeanor, had already come to accept John as her future son-in-law.

Although plans were made for a spring wedding, the marriage had to be postponed. A smallpox epidemic had broken out in Boston, where John did much of his legal work. Smallpox could be fatal, and if it wasn't fatal, the victim was often left with unsightly scars.

John chose to be inoculated, a dangerous procedure at the time. He would be infected with pus from a smallpox patient with the hope that he would catch a mild case and become immune. But there was always the possibility that inoculation would cause severe smallpox or even death. Because the patient had to be isolated for at least a month, the wedding date was set for fall.

April and May were lonely months for Abigail and John, and their letters revealed their frustration. Abigail, who now expressed herself more ardently, recalled how they had been together on the same April day the year before. She even described her restless nights. "I no sooner close my Eyes than some invisible Being . . . bears me to you."

Lysander's letters were equally ardent. "But the dear Partner of all my

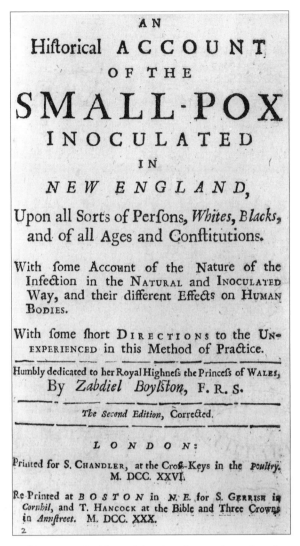

AN

Hiftorical ACCOUNT

OF THE

SMALL-POX

INOCULATED

IN

NEW ENGLAND,

Upon all Sorts of Perfons, *Whites, Blacks,* and of all Ages and Conftitutions.

With fome Account of the Nature of the Infection in the NATURAL and INOCULATED Way, and their different Effects on HUMAN BODIES.

With fome fhort DIRECTIONS to the UN-EXPERIENCED in this Method of Practice.

Humbly dedicated to her Royal Highnefs the Princefs of WALES, By *Zabdiel Boylfton,* F. R. S.

The Second Edition, Corrected.

LONDON:

Printed for S. CHANDLER, at the Crofs-Keys in the *Poultry.* M. DCC. XXVI.

Re-Printed at *BOSTON* in *N. E.* for S. GERRISH in Cornhil, and T. HANCOCK at the Bible and Three Crowns in Annftreet. M. DCC. XXX.

2

John put his life at risk when he was inoculated
for smallpox in Boston.

Joys and sorrow, in whose Affections, and Friendship I glory . . . comes into my Mind very often and makes me sigh," he wrote from his Boston hospital bed.

John and Abigail, especially John, were eager to examine their faults as a way of self-improvement. At John's urging, Abigail sent him a list of his shortcomings: "As a critic I fear you more than any other person on

Earth, and it's the only character in which I ever did, or ever will fear you." She continued, "Sometimes you know, I think you are too severe, and that you do not make quite as many allowances as Human Nature requires." She then congratulated herself on having had the courage to criticize him.

In contrast to Abigail's mild reproaches, John's list was long and detailed. Abigail was a poor card player; she had never learned to sing properly; she had "a certain modesty, sensibility, bashfulness" rather than a natural and easy manner; she did not sit erect as she should but hung her head so that her "sweet smiles" and the "bright sparkles" of her eyes were lost on others; she sat with her legs crossed, which "ruins the figure" and "injures the Health"; and she walked with her toes turned in like a parrot.

Abigail's sense of humor saved what might have become a serious lovers' quarrel. John shouldn't complain about her singing, she retorted, as she had a voice as "harsh as the screech of a peacock." Furthermore, "a gentleman has no business to concern himself about the Legs of a lady." As for her parrot-toed walk, only "Dancing School" could cure that! All in all, Abigail didn't take her faults very seriously. "Lysander must excuse me if I still persist in some of them," she teased.

In late May, John's inoculation was safely over, although the procedure had loosened his teeth, which gave him lifelong trouble. The couple were elated to be reunited. They were as drawn to each other, John observed, as were "steel and the magnet." And Abigail agreed.

That spring and summer, John worked on the Braintree property that his father had willed to him. As soon as he and Abigail were married, the young couple would move into the little saltbox house that was only a few yards away from John's birthplace, where his mother and brother Peter still lived.

Farming had always appealed to John, and he mended and built fences, planted a vegetable garden and drained a swamp. That same summer, Abigail interviewed servant girls, sewed her trousseau, shopped in Boston and was honored at female-only gatherings.

In September John was away on court business for two weeks. "Oh my dear Girl, I thank Heaven that another Fortnight will restore you to me—after so long a separation. My soul and Body have been thrown into Disorder, by your Absence," he fretted.

From the time he was young the state of his health had been a concern to John, who predicted an early death for himself. A month before the wedding he grumbled that the lengthy wait to be married had given him "a disordered stomach, a pale Face, an Aching Head and an Anxious Heart."

The long wait had taken its toll on Abigail, too. Her health was fragile at best, and she was prone to colds, influenza, migraines and insomnia. During those frustrating months of expectation and anticipation, she had become so "extremely weak" and "low spirited" that a doctor ordered her to bed until she regained her strength.

At last both John and Abigail were recovered. Abigail wrote John that she had sent her purchases to Braintree from Boston. The rest of her things would be ready in a week or two. "And then, Sir," she added, "you may take me."

On October 25, 1764, the Reverend William Smith performed the wedding ceremony in the Smiths' Weymouth home. Two and a half weeks before Abigail's twentieth birthday, and the week after John turned twenty-nine, John Adams and Abigail Smith pledged themselves to each other, dear friends and partners for life.

Chapter 2
Mamma and Pappa

After John and Abigail's wedding, they traveled the four miles from Weymouth to their Braintree home. Their modest hundred-year-old saltbox had four rooms downstairs, two bedrooms upstairs and two smaller rooms tucked under the eaves. The land covered ten acres at the foot of Penn's Hill, with an additional thirty acres nearby.

Although John converted the front room into his law office, at heart he was a farmer. In his spare time he plowed, planted, pruned trees, mended fences, carted dung, cleared out brush, dug up stones, built walls and cut ditches.

Abigail's mother had tutored her daughters in keeping house. Abigail had learned to cook, sew, bake, churn butter, preserve fruits and vegetables, smoke fish and meats, feed livestock and tend gardens. She found special pleasure in her blooming April daffodils, which she called daffies, and her early spring crops of asparagus and peas.

Any free time Abigail and John could spare was spent together. They took long hikes and often climbed Penn's Hill for a view of the ocean some two miles away. On a clear day they could see Boston, twelve miles distant, where they shopped for supplies not available in Braintree. When their chores were finished in the wintertime, they whiled away their evenings reading and talking over the day's events in front of a blazing fire.

On July 14, 1765, Abigail gave birth to their first child, a fine healthy daughter. Abigail's father baptized the infant Abigail, though she was always known as Nabby. Overjoyed, Abigail wrote a friend that Nabby's "pretty Smiles already delight my Heart, who is the Dear image of her still Dearest Pappa."

But Abigail was often lonely. As John's law practice grew, he spent more and more time at court in Boston. And his Maine–to–Cape Cod court circuit kept him on the road one week out of every four. Abigail and her sister Mary were especially close, but Mary and her husband, Richard Cranch, had recently moved from Braintree to Salem, twenty-five miles away. Although Abigail had counted on spending Thanksgiving with the

Abigail and John's first home was a little saltbox
in Braintree, Massachusetts (left), next door to John's birthplace.

Cranches in their new home, John pleaded too many court cases to take time off.

The following year Abigail and John traveled twice to Salem with Nabby. Before their first visit, John announced to the Cranches that he slept until eight or nine in the morning and wouldn't be rising at four A.M. as Richard did. His lazy habits, he explained, were the fault of his "Squeamish Wife," who kept their bedroom shutters closed until late in the morning. To prepare Mary and Richard for their second visit, Abigail wrote, "My Good Man is so very fat . . . I am lean as a rail."

While in Salem, twenty-two-year-old Abigail and thirty-one-year-old John had their portraits painted. Abigail's likeness revealed a confident and mature young woman, with a serene expression and intelligent dark eyes. Yet her upturned mouth hinted at the mischievous girl she said she had been in her "early, wild, and giddy days."

Though Abigail's portrait captured her personality, John's did not. The artist portrayed John with a smooth, round face and plump contours that made him appear soft and flabby. His bland, lackluster expression showed little vigor or character.

No one who knew John Adams would have accused him of being bland or having little character. Instead, John was willful, proud, opinionated, intense—a man of fierce honesty and honor. He may have been plump, but he was anything but soft. In his youth he had skated, sledded, swum, hunted, fished and wrestled with his friends and two brothers, Peter and Elihu. As an adult, he found his greatest pleasure in strenuous farm labor.

Nabby was almost two when Abigail and John's second child was born on July 11, 1767. He was named for Abigail's grandfather, John Quincy, who died a few days after little Johnny's birth. Just as Abigail's mother had taught her daughter how to keep house, she had also made sure Abi-

Benjamin Blyth drew Abigail's and John's likenesses in 1766 during a visit with Mary and Richard Cranch in Salem.

gail knew how to tend and care for infants. Still, Abigail was delighted when John's growing law practice allowed them to hire more help.

When John traveled from one district court to another, Abigail took over the house and farm. She gave orders to the workers, was in charge of the livestock and dairy, and handled the family finances. She was so efficient that John was only half joking when he remarked that the neighbors might judge Mrs. Adams to be a more competent manager than Mr. Adams.

No matter how long her working hours, Abigail never neglected her letter writing. She simply rose earlier and went to bed later. She wrote almost every day to John when he was away, as well as to family and friends. Although she called herself a "very incorrect writer," her appealing and natural style reflected her warmth, humor and spicy opinions.

Being busy did little to cure Abigail's loneliness when John was in Boston or riding the circuit. Sundays were the hardest. Sunday "seems a more lonesome day to me than any other when you are absent," she told

With British ships anchored in the harbor, Boston was a busy seaport city.

her husband. And she wasn't above using the children to make her point. When Johnny was several months old, she wrote to John: "Our Daughter rocks him [Johnny] to Sleep, with the Song of 'Come, Pappa, come home to Brother Johnny.'"

When Johnny was a year and a half old, Abigail and John's third child was born on December 28, 1768. Although they named the infant Susanna after John's mother, she was called Suky. An indifferent eater, Suky failed to gain weight and thrive the way Nabby and Johnny had. An anxious Abigail nursed Suky through one illness after another. John was anxious, too. When Suky was six months old, he added a special note in a letter to Abigail. "Kiss little Suky, for me," he directed.

All of Abigail and John's love and care were to no avail. On February 4, 1770, thirteen-month-old Suky died. Her grieving parents were so devastated that neither of them could write about their loss until many years later. It was one of the few times in Abigail's life when she penned almost no letters at all.

The birth of a healthy son, Charles, on May 29, 1770, some three months after Suky's death, helped to raise Abigail's and John's spirits. "Every word and action of these little creatures, twines around one's heart," Abigail confessed to Mary.

Although Abigail occasionally visited her parents in Weymouth without the children, they were never far from her mind. "I feel gratified with the imagination at the close of the Day in seeing the little flock around you inquiring when Mamma will come home," she wrote to John.

Yet, entwined as she was with the children, Abigail's thoughts occasionally traveled beyond the nursery, and she sometimes recalled the freedom she had once enjoyed with "painful pleasure." She begged her cousin to relate all he saw on his visit to England. "From my Infancy I have always felt a great inclination to visit the Mother Country," she told him with a touch of envy. "Had nature formed me of the other Sex, I should certainly have been a rover."

It was John rather than Abigail who became the rover. As he neared his thirty-sixth birthday, he concluded that his life was more than half over. But he hadn't begun to accomplish all he had set out to do! By the end of May 1771, he had grown so troubled and depressed that his doctor recommended he take a pleasure trip through Connecticut to regain his health.

John started out reluctantly. For him, doing nothing was worse than overworking, and he was unhappy and homesick. "I want to see my Wife, my Children, my Farm, my Horse, Oxen, Cows, Walls, Fences, Workmen, Office, Books and Clerks," he complained in his diary. Long before his tour was over, he turned around and headed home.

Abigail enthusiastically welcomed back her "Good Man." The following year a third son, Thomas Boylston, was born on September 15, 1772. In eight years of marriage, Abigail had given birth to five infants, four of whom survived.

Right from the beginning, Abigail was concerned about her children's morals and education. "I have an important trust committed to me," she declared. She set great store by the theory that children's minds and hearts should be shaped and guided. She believed that mothers could influence the world by raising virtuous and educated citizens, and that included daughters as well as sons. Ignoring the role of heredity or chance, she wrote, "In youth the mind is like a tender twig, which you may bend as you please." As time went on, Abigail often referred to her four children as "tender twigs."

John was also concerned. "The education of our children is never out of my mind," he wrote to Abigail. But money was a concern, too. "In a little while Johnny must go to College, and Nabby must have fine Clothes," he fussed in a letter to his brother-in-law, Richard Cranch. "Aye, and there must be dancing Schools and Boarding Schools and all that."

John was confident that Abigail was capable of overseeing the children's morals and education when he was gone. But he took no chances, and his letters were filled with advice, especially for the boys. "Fix their Attention upon great and glorious objects, root out every little Thing, weed out every meanness, make them great and manly," he directed. Abigail should see to their physical well-being, too. They must develop "strength, activity and vigor of body."

From their earliest days, the Adams children were aware of Mamma's and Pappa's zeal for books and learning. Abigail once asked what gifts they would like when their father returned from a trip. Because they knew books were what he would bring, they decided it made sense to get books that they wanted. Thomas asked for a picture book, while Charles chose a history.

Those first ten years of John and Abigail's life together were full and hectic. The children were demanding of time, effort and money. John, whose law practice kept him busy, had also become active in Patriot causes. With a note of nostalgia, he reminded Richard Cranch of the days when they were both wooing the Smith sisters; those "pleasanter Times of courtship at Weymouth," he called them.

On the other hand, in a letter to her sister Mary, Abigail viewed marriage with humor. "We do pretty much as We used to of old. Marry and give in Marriage, increase and multiply all in the old-fashioned way."

It was true that John and Abigail were no longer the lovesick Diana and Lysander they had once been. Together they had experienced births, the death of a child, illnesses, frequent separations, the nurture of four lively children and occasional misunderstandings. But with mutual love, friendship and support, John and Abigail had forged their marriage into an unbreakable union that would carry them safely through the rocky shoals that lay ahead.

Chapter 3
Fellow Patriots

John and Abigail's first years of marriage were spent raising their children and running the farm. At the same time John was working to establish his law practice. During those busy years Great Britain was tightening her grip on the thirteen American colonies.

In 1765 Great Britain passed the Stamp Act, which taxed Americans on newspapers, legal documents, college diplomas and other printed matter. When Bostonians rioted in protest, Great Britain shut down the Boston courts. With the courts closed, John's law practice evaporated. The Stamp Act, John fumed, would bring about his "ruin, as well as that of America."

John picked up an angry pen and composed instructions for the Braintree delegates to present to the colonial Massachusetts legislature, which was called the General Court. He denounced the Stamp Act with such fire that forty Massachusetts towns adopted what became known as the Braintree Instructions. Suddenly John was enjoying a wider reputation than he had ever known as a lawyer.

Facing open defiance, Great Britain repealed the Stamp Act in 1766. To celebrate, Bostonians rang bells, fired cannons and lit candles in their windows. Abigail, who had caught the whooping cough from Nabby, was

Angry Bostonians rebelled against the Stamp Act.

Death to the Stamp Act!

disappointed to miss the excitement. John was more than disappointed. He was annoyed that he hadn't received proper credit for his role in bringing down the Stamp Act.

Great Britain continued to squeeze the colonies. In 1767 the Townshend Duties taxed tea, glass, paper and the lead used in paint. Americans everywhere boycotted English goods. They dressed in homespun, brewed substitutes for tea and used colonial-made paper in a style of living that Abigail called a "Simplicity of Manners."

As soon as the courts reopened after repeal of the Stamp Act, John's law practice started up again. But he soon tired of the twelve-mile ride between Braintree and Boston. In April 1768 John rented a house in Boston on Brattle Square, and the family moved into what was then known as the White House.

Abigail was delighted. Mary and Richard Cranch now lived in Boston, too. Furthermore, Boston was a bustling town of fifteen thousand with all kinds of shops and wares that were unavailable in Braintree. And Boston published four weekly newspapers.

Abigail had earlier written to Mary: "What care I for Newspaper Politics?" But recent political issues had turned Abigail into an avid reader of current events. She even wrote John during one of his court circuit trips: "If you have any news in Town which the papers do not communicate, pray be so good as to Write it."

Once his family was settled in Boston, John became increasingly active in Patriot causes. In 1767, the Stamp Act had been replaced by new taxes called the Townshend Duties, rekindling colonial protests. Although both John and Abigail opposed violence, he began to attend meetings of the Sons of Liberty, a newly formed radical Patriot group led by his cousin Samuel Adams. Abigail welcomed John's Sons of Liberty friends to the White House—Sam Adams, John Hancock, James Otis and Dr. Joseph Warren, who became the Adamses' family doctor.

John and Abigail had lived in Boston only six months when three regiments of British soldiers occupied the city to prevent violence and restore order. The unhappy Adamses were awakened daily at dawn as the soldiers beat their drums, played their shrill fifes and exercised right beneath the White House windows. Tensions rose as gangs of youths taunted the red-coated soldiers. In turn, the soldiers used their bayonets to threaten the troublemakers.

Over the next two years John, Abigail and the children moved twice more into rented Boston homes. Those two years saw the mood in Boston grow uglier. On March 5, 1770, the city's fire bells clanged. John, who was attending a meeting at a friend's home, rushed into the icy streets, alarmed that his house might be on fire. Weaving past British soldiers armed with fixed bayonets, he ran home. Abigail and the children were equally worried about John. What a relief to find that all were safe!

Other Bostonians weren't so lucky. The fire bells had signaled trouble, not a fire. Young rowdies had shouted curses at a column of soldiers and pelted them with snowballs and rocks. Panicked, the soldiers had fired

Paul Revere's historically inaccurate engraving of the Boston Massacre inflamed public opinion against the British.

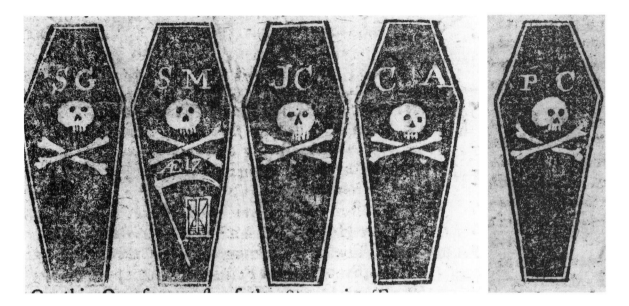

British soldiers killed five Bostonians on March 5, 1770.

into the crowd, killing five citizens and wounding six. The incident quickly became known as the Boston Massacre.

John, who believed that every person was entitled to a fair trial, agreed to defend the British soldiers. Met by a storm of criticism, John was called a traitor, and worse, by patriotic Bostonians. Hoping that tempers would cool down, British authorities delayed the trial.

In June 1770 John was elected to serve in the Massachusetts General Court. He knew that if he served in the colonial legislature, the time he spent away from his law practice would mean a serious loss of income. And it would be a commitment to become more active politically. Although John was still willing to work with the British for reforms, some of the more radical General Court representatives were already talking about independence. But that kind of talk was treasonous!

When John told Abigail that he had accepted the General Court post, she "burst into a flood of Tears." Even though women couldn't vote, hold office or attend town meetings, Abigail had become as committed to the Patriot cause as John. She now called Great Britain "that Cruel Country." Despite her fears, she agreed with John's decision. "She was very sensible of all the Danger to her and our Children as well as to me," John wrote, "but she thought I had done as I ought; she was very willing to share in all that was to come."

The trial of the British soldiers finally began in October 1770. Contrary to what everyone expected, John won the soldiers a light sentence. But in addition to his trial work, John was carrying a heavy load both at his law practice and at General Court, and he was exhausted. In the spring of 1771 he collapsed with lung and chest pains that he was sure were life-threatening.

A wise friend pinpointed John's problem. "You will never get your Health, until your Mind is at ease," he told John, and John agreed. He would simplify his life and move back to "still, calm, happy Braintree" with his family. "Farewell politics," he announced.

John's moods had always been mercurial. He soared to triumphant heights one day and then plummeted to the depths the next. He was either filled with self-confidence or riddled with self-doubt. "Ballast is what I want," he had written as a young man. "I totter with every breeze. My motions are unsteady."

Ballast and balance were what his "dear friend" gave him. Abigail was steady, calm and supportive. "I am not Naturally of a gloomy temper," she declared. She soothed John's doubts and lifted his spirits when they were low. Although she may have preferred to stay in Boston, in April 1771 she moved back to Braintree with John and the children.

But once again John grew weary of the round-trip ride between Braintree and his law practice in Boston. In November 1772 John, Abigail, Nabby, Johnny, Charles and the newest baby, Tommy, returned to

Boston, this time to a house they bought on Queen Street. With the repeal of the Townshend Duties, Boston had recently been peaceful. John was determined to devote himself solely to his family and the law. His "Heart [was] at Home."

The following year, Abigail met Mercy Otis Warren, the wife of the radical Patriot James Warren. The mother of five sons, Mercy was a published poet, political writer and playwright. Although she was sixteen years older than Abigail, the two women struck up a spirited friendship.

Abigail admired Mercy for putting her husband and children first, while at the same time moving beyond the limits of wife and mother. Abigail and Mercy both believed that women should study and read history, philosophy, biography, travel and religion. When Abigail and her "Worthy Friend" were unable to visit each other, they exchanged letters, expressing their views on all sorts of intellectual subjects, as well as on the latest fashions. One of their favorite topics was how best to raise their "tender twigs."

Abigail's new friend, Mercy Otis Warren, a talented writer and a dedicated Patriot, was portrayed by John Singleton Copley.

Dressed as Mohawk Indians, Boston rebels dumped thousands of pounds of tea into Boston Harbor.

The Adamses found life in Boston pleasant, at least for a while. But in 1773 Great Britain passed the Tea Act, which awarded its East India Company the exclusive right to sell tea in the colonies. Tea was a staple of colonial life, and American tea drinkers were furious. How dare the British dictate from whom they could buy their tea and tax them on it as well!

On December 16, 1773, a mob of Bostonians made up as Indians boarded three British ships in Boston Harbor and tossed more than three hundred chests of tea into the bay. John's retreat from politics came to an end. Although he was in Plymouth on court business at the time, he called the deed "magnificent." He viewed the Boston Tea Party as a turning point in America's relations with Great Britain. "The die is cast," he wrote the next day. "The people have passed the river and cut away the bridge."

Abigail viewed the Boston Tea Party as a turning point, too. "The flame is kindled and like Lightning it catches from Soul to Soul," she wrote to Mercy Warren.

All around them, the city of Boston was in turmoil. As punishment for the Boston Tea Party, Great Britain passed the Coercive Acts in May 1774. The port of Boston was closed to shipping. British military power was expanded at the same time that colonial self-rule was slashed, with General Thomas Gage appointed the British governor of Massachusetts. Declaring martial law in Boston, Gage brought eleven British regiments into the city to maintain order.

Although the Coercive Acts were aimed at Massachusetts, the other colonies worried that their liberties would be stripped away, too. Patriots in Williamsburg, Virginia, issued a call for delegates from all the colonies to assemble for a congress in Philadelphia. The General Court elected John Adams as a Massachusetts delegate to the First Continental Congress, to be held September 1774. John's response was heartfelt. He declared that he would "swim or sink, live or die, survive or perish with my country."

John and Abigail locked up their Queen Street home in Boston. They had to leave many of their belongings behind as John moved his family back to Braintree "to prepare for the Storm that was coming."

While John was gone, Abigail and the children would live on the farm, which had expanded considerably. When his widowed mother had remarried, John bought the family homestead next door from his brother Peter. The property covered thirty-five acres, with eighteen additional acres nearby. Four children to raise alone and full care of the two properties was a heavy responsibility for Abigail, who was not yet thirty.

Although John had confidence in Abigail's abilities, he couldn't resist giving advice. "I entreat you to rouse your whole attention to the family, the stock, the Farm, the Dairy," he wrote before leaving. Not least of all, she was to keep careful watch on the family finances. But John also expressed a more important sentiment. "I must entreat you, my dear Partner, in all the Joys and Sorrows, Prosperity, and Adversity of my Life, to take Part with me in the Struggle. I pray God for your Health."

In his letter John made it clear that he was well aware that Abigail's role was as important as his. Without her support, he wouldn't have been free to leave home. For her part, Abigail was eager to support John in every way she could so that he could represent Massachusetts at the congress.

Abigail and John were equal partners. They were partners in raising their children. They were partners in sharing their joy in good times and upholding each other in times of sorrow. Now they would be partners in sharing their talents to serve the country they loved.

Chapter 4
The Letter Writers

⧂⧂⧂⧂⧂⧂⧂⧂⧂⧂⧂⧂⧂⧂⧂⧂⧂

On a hot and dusty August 10, 1774, Abigail bid John farewell as he and the three other Massachusetts delegates headed for Philadelphia to serve in the First Continental Congress. It would be a long and tiresome journey.

The following week Abigail poured out her loneliness to John. "It seems already a month since you left me," she wrote. "The great anxiety I feel for my Country, for you and for our family renders the day tedious, and the night unpleasant." Lonely or not, Abigail was proud of her husband. "I long impatiently to have you upon the Stage of action," she added.

In his first letter home, John sent love to the family, regards to relatives and friends and impressions of his trip. It was no surprise to Abigail that he also added lengthy instructions about the children, the farm, the help and expenses.

The mail, which took at least two weeks to travel between them, was as much of an event for the children as it was for Abigail. John would have laughed to see them run for his letters "like chickens for a crumb when the Hen clucks," their mamma wrote.

John's opening words to Abigail were almost always "My Dear," while Abigail usually began her letters "Dearest Friend" and now signed herself "Portia." In ancient Rome, Portia had been the long-suffering, patient wife of the great Roman statesman Brutus. Abigail filled her loving letters with family news and reports of the farm. She also kept her husband up-to-date on political and military events as they unfolded in Boston.

John, who came to count on her keen observations, saved all her letters. In turn, he asked her to save his. Harvard-educated John Adams was the first to admit that his unschooled wife was the superior writer. "I really think that your Letters are much better for preserving than mine," he acknowledged graciously.

For his part, John kept Abigail informed about what was happening in Philadelphia. Although he promised to share a "complete History" of his experiences, he would have to wait and tell her some of it in person. The British intercepted the delegates' letters when they could.

At first John was awestruck. "This will be an assembly of the wisest men upon the continent," he crowed. But he was soon describing the frustration of being unable to get anything done. And the debates were endless, the "nibbling" and "quibbling," as he called it. "Tedious indeed is our business—slow as snails," he complained.

Occasionally John left out too much. When he wrote Abigail in October 1774, he didn't mention their upcoming tenth wedding anniversary. Instead, his letter was filled with grievances. "I am wearied to Death with the Life I lead," he grumbled. "Business is drawn out and spun out to an immeasurable Length."

In contrast, Abigail's anniversary letter was passionate. "My Much Loved Friend I dare not express to you at 300 miles distance how ardently I long for your return," she confessed. The thought "plays about my Heart, unnerves my hand while I write, awakens all the tender sentiments that years have increased and matured."

Their anniversary had come and gone by the time John returned to Braintree in November 1774. Home was a welcome sight, and his family was delighted to see him. Abigail, who had put on a little weight, had never looked lovelier, the children were well, and the harvest was in.

While in Philadelphia, John had earned a reputation for his eloquent speeches. Once home, he continued to speak out. He penned twelve letters that were published in the *Boston Gazette* under the name Novanglus, meaning "New Englander." If Great Britain stopped interfering with America's internal affairs and stopped taxing the colonies, he pointed out, harmony could be restored. As a delegate to Congress, John carefully avoided the words "independence," "rebellion" or "war."

Although John was a public figure, Abigail was not. In February 1775 she wrote to Mercy Warren that the colonies should separate from Great Britain, even though it would mean war. "Poor distressed America," she observed. "It seems to me that the Sword is now our only, yet dreadful alternative."

In April 1775 swords *were* drawn, and blood was shed. A British force marched out of Boston in an attempt to seize colonial leaders and Patriot stores of arms and gunpowder in Concord. On their way, Massachusetts militiamen confronted them at Lexington. When "the shot heard round

Massachusetts militiamen caught the British
by surprise at Lexington.

the world" was fired, fighting began between the colonial militiamen and the British troops.

John's reaction was similar to Abigail's earlier remarks to Mercy Warren. He declared that the conflicts at Lexington and Concord had changed "the instruments of warfare from Pen to the Sword."

In late April 1775 John left for Philadelphia, this time as a Massachusetts delegate to the Second Continental Congress. In 1774 the delegates had debated boycotts. In 1775 they debated war. One of their first priorities was to organize a continental army. John nominated George Washington as commander in chief, a popular choice. Later that year John was a key player in establishing the American navy and the corps of marines.

Under General Gage's harsh British rule, Massachusetts was already on a wartime footing. Thousands of Bostonians fled the city. Refugees escaping the powder keg that was Boston stopped at the Adamses' farmhouse for food and shelter. Colonial soldiers in need of food, water and rest knocked daily at their door. As supplies grew scarce and expensive, Abigail spun her own cloth and made soap. Because pins were impossible to find, Abigail asked John to bring her a bundle when he returned.

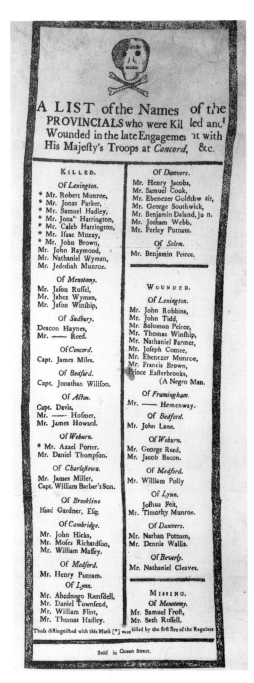

A list of Americans killed or wounded at Lexington and Concord was widely circulated.

Abigail and Johnny watched from a distance as the British attacked Breed's and Bunker Hills and burned Charlestown.

As the war grew closer to Braintree, John sent Abigail some not-very-practical advice. In case of "real Danger," he counseled from Philadelphia, "fly to the Woods with our children."

Instead, on a hot June 17, 1775, Abigail took Johnny, who was almost eight years old, up Penn's Hill to watch a battle north of Boston on Breed's Hill in Charlestown. Johnny never forgot the roar of gunfire and cannons or the sight of billowing black smoke. Americans had fortified their position on Charlestown's high ground. But after three deadly assaults, the British captured both Breed's Hill and Bunker Hill.

Abigail was devastated to see flames roar through Charlestown, her father's birthplace. She was even more devastated to learn that Dr. Joseph Warren had been killed in what came to be called the Battle of Bunker Hill. Abigail wrote to John with a "bursting Heart" that Dr. Warren, who had been the family's physician and close friend, "fell gloriously fighting for his Country."

With skirmishes breaking out and the threat of a British attack on the nearby seacoast, Abigail reported to John: "We live in continual Expectation of Hostilities." But during the long months that she and the children had endured wartime conditions, she had gained both confidence in herself and a sense of independence. "I think I am very brave upon the whole," she wrote.

"You are really brave, my dear, you are a Heroine," John agreed.

John was heroic, too. In Philadelphia he was the hardest-working member of Congress. Because the other delegates had come to depend on his judgment, intellect, character and integrity, he served on more committees than any other delegate. As chairman of twenty-five of those committees,

John and the other delegates to the Second Continental Congress met in the Pennsylvania State House.

he was in meetings from seven in the morning until eleven at night.

Although Abigail knew John was busy that spring and summer, she was unhappy with his letters. She was accustomed to descriptions of his poor health, sore eyes, bad nerves and other ailments. But now his letters were so brief and were written in such haste, she complained that about all they accomplished was to let her "know that you exist." Furthermore, he never expressed his love or feeling for her. Didn't she deserve sentiments expressed from the heart?

Luckily for John, he had already written Abigail a warm and affectionate letter before he received hers. She was delighted and thanked him for "the longest and best and most Sentimental" letter he had sent in some time. "I wrote you and made some complaints to you," she apologized, "but I will take them all back again."

To Abigail's surprise, John unexpectedly arrived home from Philadelphia in August 1775. And he had remembered to bring "two great heaps of Pins." It was a time of joy as the family was reunited. It was also a time of sorrow. A few days earlier, John's brother Elihu had died of dysentery, an intestinal disease.

Although John was home for two weeks, neither Abigail nor their "tender twigs" saw much of him. As busy with politics as ever, he spent most of his time at General Court sessions in Watertown.

John had hardly left Braintree for Philadelphia when dysentery swept the Massachusetts countryside. Abigail and three-year-old Tommy fell ill, as did two of the Adamses' servants—Patty, who died five weeks later, and Isaac, who survived. After nursing Abigail and Tommy back to health, Abigail's mother succumbed to the illness. On October 1, 1775, Elizabeth Smith died.

Aching for John's healing presence, Abigail sent him the sad news of her mother's death. She found it easier to bare her pain on paper than to give voice to her grief in person. "My pen is always freer than my tongue," she admitted. "I have written many things to you that I suppose I never could have talked."

Abigail's dearest friend may not have been by her side to console her, but his pen spoke for him. "It is very painful to be 400 Miles from one's Family and Friends when We know they are in Affliction," John sympathized. "It would be a Joy to me to fly home, to share with you your burdens and Misfortunes."

"It is a relief to one to know that we have a Friend who shares our misfortunes and afflictions," Abigail replied. "Your Letters administer comfort to my wounded Heart."

John's and Abigail's letters to each other were more than exchanges of affection, family news and political reports. They were life- and love-sustaining.

Chapter 5

Mr. and Mrs. Delegate

The gray, rainy autumn of 1775 was a dreary time for Abigail. John was gone; she was sick with jaundice, rheumatism and a bad cold; and she grieved for months over her mother's death. But she never lost interest in the fate of the nation. In her opinion, the Continental Congress delegates were too timid. They should declare independence from Great Britain. "Let us separate, they are unworthy to be our Brethren," she urged John.

Abigail was as patriotic and committed as any delegate. She called delegate Samuel Adams's wife "Sister Delegate" and referred to herself as Mrs. Delegate. After all, she had surrendered her maiden name Smith when she married, hadn't she? "Why should we not assume your titles when we give up our names?" she demanded of John.

John didn't object in the least to Abigail's calling herself Mrs. Delegate. He was proud of his patriotic and well-informed wife. "There is a Lady at the Foot of Penn's Hill who obliges me . . . with clearer and fuller intelligence than I can get from a whole Committee of Gentlemen," he boasted to a friend. And John's Philadelphia acquaintances who met Abigail on visits to Massachusetts were impressed. "An English gen-

Together the colonies would survive; separated, they would perish.

tleman says that you are the most accomplished Lady he has seen since he left England," John told her.

Abigail also acted as hostess to important visitors. When General George Washington, who was headquartered in nearby Cambridge, called on her, she found him quite charming. "The Gentleman and Soldier look agreeably blended," she reported. After a visit with Benjamin Franklin, Abigail praised him as a "true patriot."

John took a break in December and arrived in Braintree without notice just before Christmas. He was home for a month, but again spent most of his time at General Court in Watertown. At least Abigail was able to join him for a week.

A month after John left for Philadelphia in January 1776, General Washington began bombarding British-held Boston. The shelling was to divert the British so that the Americans could occupy Dorchester Heights, which was strategically located overlooking Boston and the harbor. The British returned the fire with full force.

The roar of the cannons was earsplitting. "I went to Bed after 12 but got no rest," Abigail wrote John. "The Cannon continued firing and my Heart Beat pace with them all night."

After a stressful week of constant shelling, Washington's troops took possession of Dorchester Heights and nearby Nook's Hill. They immediately dug entrenchments and fortified their position. With American cannons rimming the hills, the British could no longer defend Boston or their ships in the harbor.

On March 17, 1776, Abigail passed on stirring news to John. The British troops, as well as one thousand Bostonians loyal to the king, had evacuated Boston. From Penn's Hill she had a view of "the largest Fleet ever seen in America," as some one hundred and seventy British ships prepared to set sail for Halifax, Nova Scotia. Eight years of military rule were ended!

Abigail had more good news. The house they owned on Boston's Queen Street was in bad repair but still standing. Abigail again pressed

From Dorchester Heights, a triumphant General George Washington (on white horse) watched the British withdraw from Boston.

her husband to declare "independancy" from Great Britain. John agreed wholeheartedly. "I think you shine as a Stateswoman," he told her.

But Abigail wanted more than independence for the colonies. She urged John to consider the women. "Remember the Ladies," she entreated him. "Do not put such unlimited power into the hands of the Husbands. Remember all Men would be tyrants if they could. . . Give up the harsh title of Master for the more tender and endearing one of Friend."

Abigail wanted women to have a separate legal existence that would protect them if a husband was abusive. She wanted legal guarantees that a wife would share with her husband the profits from their mutual labors. She wanted women to have a voice in their daughters' education.

John didn't take Abigail very seriously. After all, he and Abigail were already friends and equal partners in a marriage that was unique for their time. "I cannot but laugh," he replied. Men might appear to be the masters, John teased in the same lighthearted vein, but "in Practice you know We are the subjects."

Abigail wasn't happy with John's frivolous reply. She wrote Mercy Warren that John had been very "saucy" in response to her "List of Female Grievances." She expressed her displeasure to John. "I cannot say that I think you very generous to the Ladies, for while you are proclaiming peace and good will to Men," she continued, "you insist upon retaining an absolute power over Wives." Nevertheless, in the same letter she confessed how much she missed her "dear Friend."

In Philadelphia John had little time for "remembering the Ladies." He was putting all his energies into persuading the other delegates that the colonies should separate from Great Britain. In June 1776 Congress appointed John Adams, Thomas Jefferson, Benjamin Franklin, Roger Sherman and Robert Livingston to draw up a statement declaring independence. Thomas Jefferson agreed to write the document when John declined.

The delegates (left to right) John Adams (hand in waistcoat), Roger Sherman, Robert Livingston, Thomas Jefferson, and Benjamin Franklin (seated, chin in hand), who were chosen to write the Declaration of Independence, were portrayed by Edward Savage.

In the days that followed, John was the eloquent standard-bearer in convincing reluctant delegates to vote for independence. Thomas Jefferson dubbed John "Our Colossus," while a New Jersey delegate called him "the Atlas of American independence."

On July 2, 1776, the delegates finally passed a resolution "that these united Colonies, are, and of right ought to be free and independent

States." John wrote to Abigail that July second would forever be the occasion for parades, games, sports, bells, bonfires and illuminations.

John was right about how the country would celebrate the anniversary, but he was wrong about the date. July 4, 1776, when the Second Continental Congress voted to adopt the Declaration of Independence, would forever be the honored birth date of the new nation.

Thomas Jefferson completed his rough draft
of the Declaration of Independence in less than three weeks.

Chapter 6
Public Duty, Private Tears

During the spring of 1776 a smallpox epidemic struck Massachusetts. In July Abigail arranged to be inoculated along with her children. John approved. "The Small Pox is ten times more terrible than Britons, Canadians and Indians together," he wrote. But John was in Philadelphia, while Abigail was responsible for her four sick "tender twigs."

Devoted as Abigail was to her family, she often longed for time and a room to herself. "I always had a fancy for a closet [small room] with a window which I could more peculiarly call my own," she confessed.

It was September before everyone had recovered and October before John arrived home to a warm and loving welcome. When he left for Philadelphia nine weeks later, Abigail was pregnant. With the baby due the following July, she dreaded the lonely months ahead. "This Separation is the more grievous to me than any which has before taken place," she despaired.

As the birth date drew near, Abigail experienced several frightening symptoms indicating that something was wrong, and she was concerned for the baby. "I look forward to the middle of July with more anxiety than I can describe," she confided to John.

On July 11, 1777, Abigail gave birth to a stillborn daughter, whom she had planned to name Elizabeth after her mother and grandmother. Once again, she was alone to mourn another dear one's death, this time "a sweet daughter." John, too, was alone when he received the sad news. "Never in my whole Life, was my Heart affected with such Emotions and Sensations," he grieved.

By the time John returned to Braintree in November after almost a year's absence, Abigail had regained both her health and her spirits. But soon after his arrival, he received a letter that Abigail exclaimed would "rob me of all my happiness." Congress had elected John to represent the United States in Paris. John was to replace one of three American commissioners who were negotiating a treaty with France. Their goal was to secure both French money and French troops to support the American war effort.

France! An ocean away! Abigail knew only too well that when duty beckoned, her husband would respond. However, this time would be different. She and the children would go with him.

John wouldn't hear of it. British ships patrolled the Atlantic, and the risk of capture was too great. Reluctantly, Abigail agreed to stay home. Instead, ten-year-old Johnny, who was bright, eager and mature for his age, would accompany his father. Although Abigail hated to have Johnny leave, she realized how much he would benefit from living in Paris under his father's watchful eye.

Concerned about the "many snares and temptations of Europe," Abigail instructed Johnny at length about his moral, religious, educational and physical well-being. In February 1778 she bid John and Johnny a tearful farewell as they left home to embark on the *Boston*. Just before they parted, John gave Abigail a locket with the picture of a woman watching a ship sail away. "I yield whatever is right," read the inscription.

A wintertime crossing of the Atlantic was always dangerous, especially in wartime. The *Boston* was fired on by a British ship, a cannonball

*The woman on Abigail's locket could have been Abigail herself
watching her husband's ship head for Europe.*

barely missing a direct hit on John. Father and son spent seasick days and
sleepless nights during a violent three-day storm. Lightning killed one
crew member, injured two others and split a foresail.

With Johnny in tow, John arrived in Paris on April 8, 1778, only to be
told that the commissioners had successfully negotiated a treaty with the
French government. Although France had not yet declared war on Great

Britain, part of the French fleet was already on its way to the United States. With the Treaty of Alliance signed, John wondered what was left for him to do in Paris.

Back home, Abigail and everyone else were suffering from shortages of food, clothing and provisions. Prices had soared at the same time that the value of money had plummeted. To Abigail's dismay, she hadn't received any word from John or Johnny for four months. What a relief when John's first letter arrived in June.

Soon after John and Johnny had sailed, Abigail and a Massachusetts delegate to Congress, James Lovell, had begun a correspondence. Abigail asked Lovell to send her all the news that he heard concerning John. She was also eager for him to keep her informed about what was happening in Congress.

The French fleet sailed from Europe to come to America's aid.

Lovell not only sent Abigail news, but he also began a flirtation. Although he was married, he confessed a "*secret* Admiration" for this "lovely woman." For her part, Abigail teased Lovell and called him a "very dangerous Man" and an "agreeable flatterer." She even signed her letters "Portia," the pen name she used with family and close friends. Abigail excused her more-than-friendly response to James Lovell by saying that she wrote out of love for anyone attached to her absent husband.

Three thousand miles away, John had met his counterpart, the French foreign minister, the Comte de Vergennes. Unfortunately, the two men had taken an instant dislike to each other. John wasn't getting along with the other two commissioners, either: Benjamin Franklin, who was the American minister to France, and Arthur Lee.

John especially objected to Franklin's constant partying, his open flirtations with women and his rustic-philosopher act, which came complete with a coonskin hat. He also found Franklin's casual attitude toward his diplomatic duties shocking. Most of all, he was concerned that Franklin yielded to Vergennes in all matters.

John's dislike of Franklin was tinged with jealousy. Seventy-two-year-old Franklin, who was magnetic and charming, was much in fashion with the French, while John was not. John even admitted in his diary: "I was a Man of whom Nobody had ever heard before." An earnest Yankee, he was formal, aloof and often tactless in his honesty. A friend pointed out to John how he differed from most diplomats. He didn't "dance, drink, game, flatter, promise, dress, swear with the gentlemen, and talk small talk or flirt with the Ladies."

Instead, John spent his time learning French and organizing the commission's muddled paperwork. On weekends he relaxed by exploring Paris with Johnny, who was enrolled in a nearby boarding school.

In May 1778 John wrote a letter to Samuel Adams in Congress that

The American minister to France, Benjamin Franklin, was immensely popular with the French, especially French women.

he later may well have regretted. He suggested that one commissioner could handle the work in Paris at far less expense than three. Although he hoped that the one commissioner would be himself, by November he was hearing "hints" that a change was in the air. Concerned that Congress might keep him in Europe with nothing to do, John found himself in a "State of total Suspense and Uncertainty."

With both Abigail and John under stress, the loving bond between them stretched thin. Abigail complained to John that she was hurt by his lack of attention. When she picked up her pen, she wrote, "The tears have flowed faster than the Ink." Perhaps he had "changed Hearts with some frozen Laplander." She had received only three short letters from him in the nine months since he had left. If her letters meant so little, perhaps he should let his secretary answer them.

Never one to take criticism lightly, John retorted that he was offended by his wife's "symptoms of Grief and Complaint." She should realize that he didn't dare express his feelings by mail. If the British captured a ship carrying his letters, the contents would "go into all the Newspapers of the World." Furthermore, he had written many more than three letters. Some of them must have been lost at sea.

Abigail, in turn, didn't think that John understood how difficult it was to take care of the children, manage the farm and cope with the scarcity and high cost of every necessity. To make matters worse, the Braintree snowstorms had been so severe that "Mountains of Snow" surrounded her. "How lonely are my days? How solitary are my Nights?" she demanded.

"This is the third Letter I have received in this complaining style," John scolded. "If you write me in this style I shall leave off writing entirely. . . . Am not I wretched Enough in this Banishment? What Course shall I take to convince you that my Heart is warm?"

The weeks or even months that it took for mail to arrive at its destination, if it arrived at all, worked against Abigail and John. With their letters often passing at sea, they couldn't settle differences as they arose. Instead, their anger and resentment escalated.

Then, in January 1779, James Lovell informed Abigail that Congress had elected Benjamin Franklin to be the sole commissioner in France. Even though Congress hadn't given John another assignment, Lovell assured Abigail that there was no reason for him to be upset. But Abigail knew her husband, and she knew what his reaction would be. Her heart went out to him.

John was not just upset, he was in despair. "The Scaffold is cut away, and I am left kicking and sprawling in the Mire," he wrote. He felt he had no choice but to return to Braintree with Johnny.

On August 3, 1779, John and Johnny's ship sailed into Boston Harbor. Home! The family was together for the first time in a year and a half. Misunderstandings and accusations were forgotten as Abigail and John connected with a renewed sense of intimacy. Surely, this time John was home for good.

Braintree was at its summer best. Nabby, Charles and Tommy were thriving. The farm under Abigail's care was prospering, and there were pleasant visits with family and friends. As the center of attention, Johnny showed off his fluent French and told of the sights he had seen and famous men he had met.

Soon after he arrived, John was elected as a delegate to the Massachusetts Constitutional Convention. Working out of his home, John drafted what became the core of the Massachusetts Constitution of 1780. He advocated checks and balances by separating the executive, legislative and judicial branches of government. With much of the document later used as a model for the Constitution of the United States, John considered the work to be one of his finest achievements.

John had been home only a month when he learned that Congress wanted him to return to Paris. In the event that Great Britain was willing to discuss peace, he would be the sole American minister to negotiate a treaty.

Ambitious as ever, and anxious to prove his worth after his recent humiliating experience in France, John accepted. He tried to soften the blow. "Keep up your Spirits and throw off Cares," he advised Abigail. "We shall yet be happy."

With Great Britain showing no signs of wanting to end the war, Abigail was certain that John's Paris stay would be a long one. She was also certain that keeping up her spirits and throwing off her cares would be easier said than done.

Chapter 7

A Cruel Separation

When John sailed for France on November 15, 1779, both Johnny and Charles were with him. Although neither boy had wanted to go, Abigail agreed with John that they were at an age when their father's influence was more important than their mother's. Nine-year-old Charles, who was usually a bright and cheerful child, was heartbroken. Abigail was heartbroken, too. "My dear sons I cannot think of them without a tear," she wrote the day after they left. "Little do they know the feelings of a Mother's Heart!"

But Abigail didn't give up her mother role easily, only now it would be by long distance. She cautioned Johnny to pay "strict attention and watchful care to correct" his temper. She then went on to lay a heavy burden on his twelve-year-old shoulders: "Do Honour to your Country, and render your parents supremely happy," she directed.

With only Nabby and little Tommy at home, Abigail felt "widowed." She wrote John that she suffered from "the cruel torture of Separation." The Braintree weather didn't help. "Winter set in with all its horrors in a week after you sailed," she declared. "Such mountains of snow have not been known for 60 years."

Abigail not only wrote to John and the boys, but she and James Lovell also resumed their correspondence. Lovell addressed Abigail as "charming Lady" and "most lovely of the Loveliest Sex," signing one of his letters, "I am Portia's affectionate Friend." Abigail scolded Lovell for his outrageous compliments, but she never suggested that they stop writing to each other.

Although Abigail assumed that John and the boys had arrived safely in Paris by the end of December, or January at the latest, she was mistaken. Their leaking vessel had limped into a Spanish port in December 1779 with "seven feet of Water in her Hold."

From Spain, John, Johnny, Charles and their party traveled some eight hundred miles in the dead of winter over the Pyrenees Mountains. They finally reached Paris on February 9, 1780, after a two-month journey by foot, carriage and muleback. "The Mountains—the Cold—the Mules—the Houses without Chimneys or Windows. . . . We walked, one third of the Way," an exhausted John wrote home.

At their first meeting, John and the French foreign minister, Vergennes, once again clashed. They hadn't gotten along two years before, and they didn't get along now. John wanted the

Unlike John Adams, the French foreign minister, the Comte de Vergennes, was an experienced and wily diplomat.

French to send more military aid to the United States. He was also eager to negotiate a peace settlement directly with Great Britain without the French participating as an equal partner. But direct negotiation with the British would violate the 1778 French-American Treaty of Alliance. Vergennes rejected both proposals outright.

By July 1780 John realized he wasn't getting anywhere with Vergennes. He took Johnny and Charles out of their French boarding school, and the three of them went sightseeing in Belgium and the Netherlands. For some time Congress had wanted to borrow money from the Dutch to help finance the war, and John's visit to the Netherlands gave him the opportunity to advocate for that goal. John liked the Dutch people, and the Dutch people liked him.

In August John settled his little family in Amsterdam and enrolled his sons in a Dutch boarding school. When the boarding school didn't work out, he sent them to the University of Leyden.

John spent the next year trying to convince Dutch businessmen to grant the United States a loan. But the war wasn't going well. The British had captured Charleston, South Carolina, and the southern American army was in shambles. And when Great Britain threatened to attack Dutch shipping if a loan were made to the United States, the Dutch lost all interest in granting the money. Despite having failed, in early 1781 John was named American minister to the Netherlands.

Late that spring, John's friend Francis Dana was appointed to represent the United States in Russia. Because French was spoken at the Russian court, Dana needed a French-speaking secretary who could also write. Bright, studious Johnny Adams, who was almost fourteen, fit the bill. In July 1781 he and Dana set off for Russia.

Earlier in the spring eleven-year-old Charles had been seriously ill. As the months passed he begged to go home. He didn't feel well, he missed his mother, and he was lonely without Johnny. In August John reluctantly put Charles on a ship bound for the United States in the care of a fellow passenger. Charles had charmed everyone he met in Europe, and John felt lost without his sunny, good-natured son. "He is a delightful, little fellow. I love him too much," he had written earlier to Abigail. With

John's rented house in Amsterdam overlooked a lovely tree-lined canal.

both boys gone, John mourned that he was without "the greatest pleasure I had in life, the society of my children."

John had a difficult summer all the way around. He spent two weeks in Paris discussing peace proposals with Vergennes, which turned out to be a waste of time. Then he learned that he would no longer be the sole peace commissioner in Paris. Congress had appointed four commissioners to serve with him: John Jay, Henry Laurens, Thomas Jefferson, who later declined, and John's archenemy, Benjamin Franklin. John considered Congress's decision an insult and a rejection of everything he had tried to do in Europe.

As so often happened when he was under stress, John's health failed, and he collapsed in August 1781. He was sicker than he had ever been. Although he called it a "nervous fever," it was probably malaria. He wrote Abigail that he had been "as near to death as any man could be without being grasped in his arms."

When James Lovell told Abigail that John had been stripped of his sole authority in Paris, she was almost as upset as John was. "For myself I have little ambition or pride—for my *Husband* I freely own I have much," she declared.

The year 1781 had been difficult for Abigail, too. She had learned to accept that her husband put duty to country before his family. But she was deeply distressed that she hadn't received a letter from him in a year. She began to address John as "dear absent Friend." She'd had no word from Johnny in Russia, either. And although she knew that Charles was on his way home, she had heard nothing except frightening rumors about the fate of his ship.

Money was tight, and John's salary barely covered basics. To pay the sky-high taxes, Abigail sold luxuries that John sent to her from Europe. Gloves, ribbons, fans, pins, china, linens, handkerchiefs, tea, calico, carpets and more arrived by the trunk- and crateful for her to sell. Abigail also ministered to John's family when his sister-in-law, stepfather and brother's infant daughter died. For weeks she had tended her ill mother-in-law. Enough was enough. How long did John expect her to endure this "cruel State of Separation"?

"I am," she wrote across the miles, "much afflicted with a disorder called the *Heartache*."

Chapter 8

Indecision

As difficult as 1781 was for both John and Abigail, news about the war lifted their spirits. Combined American and French forces won an overwhelming victory at Yorktown, Virginia. The British surrendered on October 19, 1781.

Abigail's spirits soared even higher when Charles arrived safely home in January 1782 after a five-month journey. But Charles passed on alarming news. During a long layover that his ship had made in Spain, he heard that his father was terribly sick in Amsterdam. Abigail hadn't yet received John's letter telling her of his collapse. It was too much to bear! Five months later, she was just learning that her husband was critically ill!

But back in Europe, John had recovered and was doing well. The American victory marked a turning point in relations with the Dutch. In April 1782 the Dutch government formally recognized John Adams as United States ambassador, and John moved from Amsterdam to The Hague, the Netherlands' seat of government.

Two months later John closed the first of four Dutch loans to the United States that would eventually total three and a half million dollars. At last he was receiving the recognition that he felt he deserved. "Your

George Washington accepted the British surrender at Yorktown
after a decisive victory.

humble Servant has lately grown much into Fashion," he boasted to
Abigail.

Abigail replied that she was proud of John's success, but he should
remember that she had been a necessary partner. "I will take praise to
myself," she replied with a tart pen. "I feel that it is my due, for having

sacrificed so large a portion of my peace and happiness to promote the welfare of my country." She continued, "Does your Heart pant for domestic tranquility?" Back in September 1781, Abigail had suggested that she join John in Europe. "What if I should take a trip across the Atlantic?" she had queried.

John was lonely, too. "I must go to you or you must come to me. I can-

Benjamin West's painting of the preliminary peace treaty signing in Paris was never completed. (Left to right: The four American commissioners, John Jay, John Adams, Benjamin Franklin, Henry Laurens, and Franklin's son, William, secretary)

not live, in this horrid Solitude," he had responded. But now was not a good time. He had left The Hague to meet with Benjamin Franklin, John Jay, Henry Laurens and French officials in Paris to negotiate a peace treaty with the British. "I am so wedged in with Public Affairs that it is impossible to get away at present," he apologized.

An up-and-down, on-again, off-again correspondence between John and Abigail had begun. First John urged Abigail to make the long journey. "Will you come and see me?" he asked. Then he advised her not to start out. He might be recalled to the United States and they would pass each other at sea.

From Braintree, Abigail first begged John to return. Then she suggested twice more that she and Nabby travel to Europe. On their eighteenth anniversary, October 25, 1782, she reminded her "Dearest Friend" of all the precious moments between them that had been lost forever: "Who shall give me back Time . . . those *years* I cannot recall?"

When preliminary peace treaty terms were agreed on in December 1782, John wrote Abigail that it was time for him to resign his post and return to Braintree. "For the Family, and mostly for the Honour of our Country I should come home," he concluded.

But it would be another nine months before the final Treaty of Paris was signed on September 3, 1783, ending the War of Independence. By then John was reluctant to leave. With the war over, he was hoping against hope to be appointed the first American minister to Great Britain.

Several weeks after the treaty was signed, John came down with influenza. Feeling "feeble, low and drooping," he dashed off three letters in a row insisting that Abigail come to him in Paris. "I cannot be happy, nor tolerable without you," he pleaded. She could board Charles and Tommy with her sister Elizabeth and Elizabeth's teacher-husband and

Sixteen-year-old Johnny was a worldly young man when he returned from Russia.

bring Nabby with her. Besides, she would see Johnny again. After returning safely from Russia, Johnny had joined his father in Paris.

With the peace treaty signed, ships at sea were at last safe from British attack. Back in Massachusetts, Abigail's ailing father had died, and Abigail, who had been nursing him, was free to travel.

Although Abigail had earlier offered to make the trip, now she hesitated. It would mean leaving Charles and Tommy for what might be a long time. She had never been more than fifty miles from Braintree, and she pictured herself as an "awkward figure" at the courts of Europe. Plus, she dreaded crossing the Atlantic in wintertime. "I am so much of a coward upon the Water," she confessed to John.

But all of Abigail's concerns paled in comparison with seeing her dear friend and her eldest son again. On June 20, 1784, she set sail. With her were Nabby, who would celebrate her nineteenth birthday at sea, two servants, John Briesler and Esther Field, and a cow to provide milk for the voyage.

Abigail and John hadn't seen each other in nearly five years. They had both endured loneliness, illness, frustration, crises, disagreements and months-long silences. It was past time to pick up the tattered fabric of their marriage.

Chapter 9
Very, Very Happy

The month's voyage to England was even more unpleasant than Abigail had anticipated. For the first ten days she and Nabby were so seasick that they were confined to bed. When they felt well enough to be on deck, they had to be tied in their chairs. Rough seas or not, Abigail organized a cleanup crew to scrub the filthy cabin floors, and also taught a thing or two to the "lazy dirty" cook.

Abigail and Nabby reached London on July 21, 1784, along with their servants, John and Esther, but without the cow, which had died at sea. Johnny had been waiting a month for them in London. When they didn't arrive, he had returned to The Hague, where he was now living with his father.

As soon as John heard that his wife and daughter were in their London hotel, he wrote Abigail a jubilant letter, calling himself "the happiest Man upon Earth. I am twenty Years younger than I was Yesterday." Because he was delayed by business at The Hague, he sent Johnny back to London.

"Oh, my Mamma! and my dear Sister!" Johnny cried when he burst into their hotel room nine days later.

Abigail was both thrilled to see Johnny . . . and astonished. She had bid farewell in Braintree to a twelve-year-old boy and was now being greeted by a seventeen-year-old man of the world.

John hurried to London as soon as he was free. What an emotional as well as anxious moment! But there was no need to be nervous. In a letter to her sister Mary, Abigail wrote: "Poets and painters wisely draw a veil over those Scenes which surpass the pen of the one and the pencil of the other. We were indeed a very, very happy family once more."

John and Johnny had been to London before. They had traveled to England in October 1783 to visit the health resort in Bath, where John had hoped to regain his strength after his bout of influenza. But they had been captivated by the sights of London and had lingered in the city for two months. During their stay, American artist John Singleton Copley had painted John's portrait. Although Abigail later described the painting as "a very Elegant picture," John never liked it. Copley had portrayed him as not only learned and forceful, but also somewhat smug and self-important.

The day after John, Abigail, Johnny and Nabby were reunited in London, they started out for France in a secondhand coach that Johnny had bought. With Esther and John accompanying them, the coach was full to overflowing. But the discomfort didn't bother them. They were together again. They crossed the English Channel, then continued on to Paris. After a few days of sightseeing, they drove four miles to the mansion that John had rented in Auteuil.

Abigail soon realized that managing a forty-room country house that she described as "gay and beautiful" wasn't quite like running her little Braintree saltbox. In addition to Esther and John, six French servants were on the staff. Although Abigail could read French, she couldn't speak it, and the servants didn't speak English. Practical as ever, Abigail was annoyed that each servant had one job and one job only. The cook refused to wash dishes, the hairdresser wouldn't make the bed, and the gardener balked at running errands.

John Singleton Copley portrayed John holding the Treaty of Paris and pointing to a map of the new United States.

Abigail discovered that John didn't care much for housework, either. He had been an important statesman for too long! "He loves to have everything as it should be, but does not wish to be troubled about them," was her prickly comment to Uncle Cotton Tufts.

Nevertheless, Abigail and John settled back into each other's lives with remarkable ease. The family breakfasted together before going their separate ways. They met for dinner at two, after which John tended to official business, while Abigail read or wrote letters until teatime. In the evening the family came together again for supper. Occasionally, John and Abigail dined out or entertained guests at home.

The four Adamses drove to Paris often to enjoy what the city had to offer. Although Abigail disapproved of the French celebration of food, wine, gambling, dancing, flirting, balls and parties, she relished the wonderful French world of theater, museums, opera and ballet. "If you ask me what is the Business of Life here, I answer Pleasure," she reported to Mercy Warren.

Abigail was especially fond
of French theater.

Although Abigail was alarmed at first by the boldness of French women, she soon came to admire their learning, taste and open, frank manner. Always a champion of education for women, she was impressed by how well informed French women were, and she envied the way they expressed their opinions freely, speaking out with intelligence and assurance.

But Abigail missed her sisters, Mary and Elizabeth, and her friend Mercy Warren, all of whom had supported her during John's long absences. When she met the Marquise de Lafayette, she was drawn to the young wife of the Revolutionary War hero. Like Abigail, the marquise was direct, energetic and dressed simply. The two women quickly struck up a warm friendship.

Thomas Jefferson became good friends with both Abigail and John during their time together in France. Portrait by Charles Willson Peale.

While Abigail adjusted to life in France, John worked with Benjamin Franklin and Thomas Jefferson, who had recently arrived in Paris. Because the United States was eager for European and African countries to open their ports to American trade, the three men had been commissioned by Congress to negotiate commercial treaties. Despite Benjamin Franklin's efforts to be cordial, John never overcame his dislike of the elder statesman.

On the other hand, John and Thomas Jefferson, who had met in 1775 at the Second Continental Congress, forged a close bond during their time in

France. Abigail was fond of Jefferson, too, and they became fast friends. Jefferson, who was a widower, was sick for most of his first year in Paris, and Abigail took him under her wing like a member of the family. She described him as "one of the choice ones of the Earth."

With only Prussia willing to open its port to American trade, the three-man commission had little success. And then, in April 1785, John received news that had been his dream and goal for more than two years. Congress had elected him to be the first American ambassador to Great Britain. Earlier John had forwarded to Congress a description of the man who would best fill the position. Not surprisingly, the description was an accurate portrait of John Adams!

Soon after John learned of his appointment, seventy-eight-year-old Benjamin Franklin, who was in poor health, requested to be sent home. In his place as American minister to France, Congress named Thomas Jefferson. Despite serving in different countries, John and Jefferson were ordered to continue negotiating commercial treaties.

Before they left for England, John and Abigail saw Johnny off to the United States. The three of them had agreed that almost eighteen-year-old Johnny, who had always excelled at his studies, should finish his education at Harvard. Much as she would miss the son with whom she had just become reacquainted, Abigail was eager for Johnny to establish a future in his own country. Nabby was especially heartbroken to part with the brother she idolized.

On May 20, 1785, John, Abigail and Nabby departed for England, once again accompanied by the loyal Esther and John. The Adamses' nine months in France had been a happy family experience. And it had given Abigail and John the time and opportunity to successfully and lovingly bridge their long, lonely years of separation.

Chapter 10
Mr. and Mrs. Ambassador

The first American ambassador to Great Britain and his wife, daughter and two servants arrived in London on May 26, 1785. The Adams family had hardly settled in their hotel before John was formally received by King George III. The meeting was emotional for both men. John represented American independence, while King George was the monarch who had lost Great Britain's most valuable piece of real estate. Despite negative newspaper reports, the king was cordial and welcoming, and John was pleased at his reception.

Unlike John, Abigail wasn't pleased with *her* encounter with royalty. At a palace reception, she and Nabby stood for four hours waiting for the king and queen to circle the crowded room to greet them. When it was finally their turn, the king asked Abigail if she had taken a walk that morning. Abigail later remarked that she was tempted to retort that she had spent the entire morning dressing and having her hair arranged to prepare for this moment. But she restrained herself and simply replied, "No, Sire."

Abigail, who took on the search for suitable quarters, found a gracious townhouse for rent on Grosvenor Square. One of the first letters she and John received in their new home was from Thomas Jefferson. "The

As America's first ambassador to Great Britain, John Adams presented his diplomatic papers to King George III in a historic meeting.

departure of your family has left me in the dumps," he lamented.

John and Jefferson continued both their business and their friendship by post. Abigail and Jefferson corresponded, too, exchanging opinions, news of political events, intellectually stimulating ideas and

John and Abigail had their portraits painted during their stay in London.

gossip about people they knew. They even shopped for each other.

During their first year in London, John, Abigail and Nabby had their portraits painted. For once John was satisfied. The artist portrayed John at fifty with a somber, dignified expression. Forty-one-year-old Abigail's

portrait revealed the same strong character and somewhat sharp features that were evident in a portrait of her father painted years before. Her eyes, however, were her own—dark, lustrous and thoughtful. Although Nabby appeared much older than twenty, John thought the artist had caught her modest manner and quiet wit.

As the ambassador's wife, Abigail became involved in John's career for the first time since he entered public life. Together they attended diplomatic dinners and receptions, with the formal birthday and anniversary celebrations at court being Abigail's least favorite affairs. Neither John nor Abigail was happy with the weight they gained from the constant round of parties, but at least Abigail viewed it with a sense of humor. She wrote her sister Mary that she pitied any horse that might have to carry the two of them.

Although Abigail dreaded her court appearances, she thoroughly enjoyed the intellectual opportunities that London offered. She declared that attending a series of science lectures "was like going into a beautiful Country, which I never saw before, a Country which our American Females are not permitted to visit or inspect."

In their free time Abigail and John toured the surrounding countryside, making a point to visit the little English town of Braintree. When John attended to diplomatic business in the Netherlands for a month, Abigail traveled with him.

John also took time off for himself. He read, studied and wrote. He worked for two years on a three-volume project in which he described past and present forms of government, as well as advocated three separate branches of government, the executive, legislative and judicial. When Thomas Jefferson was in London on business in the spring of 1786, the two men spent a week sightseeing, visiting historic sites and gardens around London.

The most personally satisfying event of the Adamses' London stay was the outcome of what John called The Family Affair. Three years earlier, back in Braintree, Nabby and dashing Royall Tyler had met and fallen in love. Abigail was opposed to the match at first. Tyler had a reputation for having squandered his inheritance, as well as being a little too interested in the local ladies. But Tyler's charm soon won Abigail over.

When John heard about the romance, he was furious at his wife for allowing their seventeen-year-old daughter to be swept off her feet. By the time John finally gave his grudging approval, Abigail and Nabby had set sail for Europe, and his letter never reached them.

With plans to marry, Nabby and Tyler corresponded for six months. And then Tyler's letters abruptly stopped. He didn't reply to Nabby's letters or to Abigail's and John's repeated questions as to his intentions. Devastated, Nabby broke their engagement.

When John's handsome secretary, Colonel William Smith, learned that Nabby was free, he began to court the shy, sensitive young woman. Abigail and John were delighted. Abigail, who described William as "a man of strict honor," encouraged the match. The young couple were married in London on June 12, 1786.

Mather Brown painted Nabby's portrait in 1765 and her husband William Smith's portrait the following year.

Meanwhile, trouble was brewing back in western Massachusetts. Farmers, unable to pay their mortgages and taxes, faced debtors prison and the loss of their farms. In December 1786 Daniel Shays led hundreds of farmers in an armed rebellion. Although the revolt was quickly crushed by the state militia, the uprising spread alarm throughout the new nation.

When word of Shays's Rebellion reached London, John and Abigail, especially Abigail, were distressed that American citizens had taken the law into their own hands. In contrast, Jefferson voiced approval. He believed that a healthy spirit of resistance was good for the country.

Despite their growing political differences, John and Jefferson remained on good terms. In December 1786 Jefferson wrote Abigail and John from Paris to ask a favor. His eight-year-old daughter, Polly, would be arriving in London in the spring. Could she stay with them until he could send for her? Abigail and John replied that they would be delighted to help out.

On June 26, 1787, a frightened Polly appeared on the Adamses' doorstep, accompanied by Sally Hemings, a fourteen-year-old Jefferson slave. Abigail and John did everything they could to entertain the unhappy child and make her feel at home. When Jefferson's French-speaking servant arrived ten days later to escort her back to Paris, Polly was desolate at leaving her new friends. "She is indeed a fine child," Abigail wrote to Jefferson.

Right from the beginning, John faced an uphill battle as ambassador, and it never got easier. The British were bitter about losing their colonies, and it was well known that John Adams had been one of the American commissioners at the peace treaty negotiations. The ruthless London press printed critical and false reports of John's activities and speeches. He had hardly arrived in London when a horrified newspaper reporter wrote: "An Ambassador from America! Good heavens what a sound!" And John was badgered constantly by American Loyalists, who claimed they were owed money for the American property they had lost when they fled to England during the war.

Although John did his best to negotiate a treaty with the British government that would open British ports to American trade, he was unsuccessful. He was also unsuccessful in convincing the British to abandon their forts in America's Northwest Territories. As a final insult, the British government refused to send an ambassador to the United States to represent Great Britain.

Abigail discovered that being on the firing line with John could be painful. As a proud woman who was a staunch defender of her husband's reputation, she took criticism of him personally. She wrote to her sister Mary that a better name for the press was "the News Liars." And unlike France, where she and the Marquise de Lafayette had become close, she found no such like-minded friend in London. Opinionated as ever, Abigail described the English as cold, haughty and full of "narrow" prejudices.

In 1787 Abigail received news that her brother, William, had died. During recent years, he had been drinking heavily, was in serious legal trouble and had abandoned his family. Abigail grieved over his sad and wasted life.

Good news also arrived. Following John and Abigail's instructions, Uncle Cotton Tufts had bought a house in Braintree for three thousand dollars. The handsome seven-room house, which was a mile and a half north of their little saltbox, sat on eighty-three acres of meadow, farmland and woods.

As time passed, Abigail suffered increasingly from rheumatism and ill health. She felt middle-aged, and she *was* middle-aged. She and John became grandparents. William Steuben Smith was born to Nabby and William in April 1787. "I am a grandmamma. A grand—oh no!" Abigail exclaimed in mock horror. "That would be confessing myself old which would be quite unfashionable and vulgar."

Having a new baby in the family made Abigail miss her own "tender twigs" all the more. Johnny had graduated Phi Beta Kappa from Harvard as a class orator without his proud mother and father in attendance. Charles and Tommy, who were now students at Harvard, had grown into young adults. Abigail hadn't seen her two younger sons in almost four years, while John hadn't seen Charles in seven years or Tommy in more than eight. Tommy so resented his parents' absence that he refused to write them.

It was time to go home. Discouraged that he couldn't accomplish his goals, John requested that Congress recall him when his term was up. With thanks to John for his "patriotism, perseverance, integrity, and diligence" in service to his country, Congress agreed.

In late April 1788 Abigail and John, along with their faithful servants, Esther and John, who were now married, began their long voyage home. Although they were returning without having achieved much success, they were returning with the bonds of their marriage strengthened. For nearly four years they had worked together as "dear partners," sharing equally in the rewards as well as the failures.

Chapter II

A Flurry of Politics

John and Abigail were astonished by the welcome they received when they sailed into Boston Harbor on June 17, 1788. Cannons were fired and church bells pealed. Governor John Hancock's representative greeted them at the gangplank as thousands of Bostonians cheered their hometown hero.

Abigail and John's first order of business was to see their children. Charles and Thomas hurried over from Harvard. John Quincy arrived a few days later from his law job north of Boston. What a reunion! So many years had passed! Their "tender twigs" were all grown up.

The second order of business was to move into their new home. Although John was delighted with it, Abigail was not. She remembered the house as being spacious, but compared to the mansions they had lived in abroad, it seemed small and dark indeed. And with the plastering, painting and carpentry work still not finished, the house was in shambles.

Abigail rolled up her sleeves and went to work. Gradually the house and gardens began to take shape under her capable hands. Meanwhile, John happily spent his time tramping over every foot of the property and

*Abigail and John were eager to get settled in their new home
on their return from Europe.*

visiting with his eighty-year-old mother, who had feared she would never
see him again.

Although John had been uncertain about his future, all the praise and
acclaim that he was receiving convinced him to stay in public life. The
new Constitution, which had been ratified on June 21, 1788, called for
the election of a president and vice president. With George Washington
the obvious choice for president, John considered himself to be the obvious choice for vice president. After all, he had headed up more committees in the Second Continental Congress than any other congressman
and had been the eloquent leader in convincing reluctant congressmen to
vote for independence. He had been a commissioner at the peace treaty

negotiations and served as the first American ambassador to both the Netherlands and Great Britain.

"We are all in a flurry of politics," John reported to Abigail several months later. Nabby had just given birth to her second son, John Adams Smith, and Abigail was on Long Island helping out. For once, Abigail was pleased that John planned to return to public life. She and Nabby missed each other, and the nation's capital was to be in New York City, only eleven miles from where Nabby and William lived.

For the country's first election, electors from the thirteen states were each to cast two votes. The Constitution called for the candidate with the most votes to become president, with the runner-up to serve as vice president, an election process that was changed to its present form in 1804.

John had advantages over his rivals, John Hancock, John Jay and George Clinton. New England's many electors backed Adams, who was known nationally as a man of integrity. And his conservative views had won him many supporters. John Adams, it was said, would be "safe."

To no one's surprise, George Washington was elected president unanimously. John came in second, with thirty-four votes out of sixty-nine. Rather than being elated at winning the vice presidency, John, being John, was crestfallen that he hadn't received more votes.

With Abigail staying in Braintree to oversee work on their house, John set off for New York on April 13, 1789. Eight days later he was inaugurated vice president of the United States in a simple ceremony witnessed by members of the Senate. In contrast, on April 30, George Washington was inaugurated president on the balcony of Federal Hall to the cheers and applause of hundreds of spectators.

John could hardly wait for Abigail to join him in New York. In letter after letter he urged her to hurry. But Abigail wouldn't be rushed. She had to pack her belongings, ship furniture, write orders for the farmworkers and close up the house. Accompanied by Charles and her brother's young daughter, Louisa, who now lived with them, Abigail arrived in late June.

John had rented an elegant mansion with a spectacular view of the Hudson River and New Jersey. Abigail called the setting "the most delicious spot I ever saw." Nabby, with her little family, planned to stay with her parents, as did Charles, who had just graduated from Harvard.

Although they could count on the reliable John and Esther Briesler, finding other servants was a problem. Like the Washingtons, the Adamses were expected to entertain often and well. With their busy social life, the purchase of a coach and feeding a houseful of family, guests and servants, John and Abigail worried about money. And it didn't help when they learned that George Washington's salary was $25,000 a year while John's was $5,000!

Newly sworn-in Vice President John Adams (hat under his arm) witnessed George Washington's inauguration as president.

The vice presidency had other drawbacks. John's official duty was to preside as president of the Senate and cast a vote in case of a tie. John had always had a knack for irritating people, and he soon irritated the senators. He lectured them as if they were children, explained the law they were to vote on and then told them how to vote.

John further annoyed the senators by suggesting that George Washington's title should be "His Highness, the President of the United States of America, and Protector of the Rights of the Same," with "His Highness" at the very least. John believed that titles and formalities encouraged respect.

Political opinion was that John's ten years abroad had turned him into a monarchist, or king lover. And his powdered wig, ceremonial sword and ornate coach only confirmed that impression. A hostile editor dubbed John with a title of his own, "His Rotundity."

Although John was not a king lover, his exposure to the royal courts of Europe *had* affected him. The earlier fires of his Revolutionary spirit had waned and he had become increasingly conservative. In a series of newspaper essays, he expressed disapproval of the 1789 French Revolution and its mob rule, advocating instead a powerful central government and strong presidency that would control such radical behavior. He also observed that citizens were not all equal. Those citizens who were educated and talented were a source of stability in society.

In contrast, Secretary of State Thomas Jefferson and his followers, who had earlier praised Shays's Rebellion, were enthusiastic supporters of the French Revolution. They championed a weak central government that would allow the people to govern themselves. As two distinct political parties began to form, John Adams and Thomas Jefferson's once warm friendship cooled.

On the other hand, the Washingtons and the Adamses got along well. Even though the president almost never consulted his vice president,

John held him in high regard. He said that the president had "talents of a very Superior kind," adding, "I wish I had as good."

Abigail, who regarded Martha Washington with the same kind of respect, described her as a "most friendly, good Lady, always pleasant and easy." John even had portraits painted of the Washingtons, which he later hung in his home.

In November 1790 the nation's capital was moved from New York City to Philadelphia. All sorts of family arrangements had to be made as

John paid forty-three dollars for Edward Savage's portraits of George and Martha Washington, which he hung in the dining room at Peacefield.

Abigail once again packed up. Charles would move in with Nabby and William, while eighteen-year-old Thomas would live with his parents and study law.

Soon after they arrived in Philadelphia, Thomas fell seriously ill with what his mother called "acute rheumatism," but which was probably rheumatic fever. Abigail and John were concerned about Thomas's persistent rheumatism and frequent depressions.

They were concerned about their other "tender twigs," too. Nabby and William were heavily in debt as William pursued one unsuccessful business scheme after another. And Nabby and William's third son, Thomas Hollis, was a sickly baby.

Although twenty-three-year-old John Quincy was a practicing lawyer, he was still financially and emotionally tied to his parents. And he was despondent and uncertain about his future. He had recently broken up with a young woman he had planned to marry—after his mother had pointed out that he was not yet in a position to support a wife.

Abigail described Charles, who was a troubled young man, as "not at peace with himself." To his parents' dismay, Charles had been a heavy drinker at Harvard and had done little to curb his drinking since. In the back of their minds was the memory of the death of Abigail's brother from drinking.

Peaceful Braintree was a welcome sight when Abigail and John returned in May 1791. But Abigail fell ill again, this time with ague, a malarial fever that left her weak and sickly all summer.

Neither Abigail's health nor frame of mind was improved by the capital's social demands when she and John returned to Philadelphia in October. She was expected to make and receive calls every day but Sunday. She and John hosted an open house, or levee, on Mondays and a formal dinner on Wednesdays. Receptions, teas, parties and balls filled up the rest of her calendar. "I have so little time to call my own," she complained to Mary.

In February 1792 Abigail took to her bed for six weeks with rheumatism and a relapse of the ague. Although she wanted desperately to return home, she was so "feeble and faint" that she and John didn't start out for two months. But home was no longer in Braintree. Their section of Braintree had been split off into a new town named Quincy in honor of Abigail's grandfather John Quincy.

Abigail told John in the fall that they could no longer afford two households, one in Quincy and one in Philadelphia. And she claimed that Philadelphia's climate was harmful to her health. She wouldn't be returning to the capital ever again. When John left for Philadelphia in November, Abigail stayed in Quincy.

Alone in the capital, John's routine didn't change. He grumbled to Abigail of his "tedious days and lonely nights." Although he talked about resigning the vice presidency, he was a realist. George Washington was certain to win the upcoming 1792 election. If John wanted to run for president in 1796, he would have to serve as Washington's vice president for a second term. And that meant four more years of presiding over the Senate.

In the end, John's lifelong craving for recognition won out. He announced that he would be a candidate for vice president in the 1792 election. To change his monarchist image, John abandoned his powdered wig, ceremonial sword and handsome coach.

As expected, George Washington was unanimously elected president for a second term. Although John won the next highest number of votes to be reelected vice president, the margin was narrower than it had been in 1789, seventy-seven votes out of 132. The die was cast. All John had to look forward to was four more years of politics as usual . . . without his best friend beside him.

Chapter 12

Turnabout

An unhappy John knew just what to expect of his job when his second term began in March 1793. The vice presidency, he declared, was "the most insignificant office that ever the Invention of man contrived." What John didn't expect was how much he would miss Abigail. He begged her to join him. If only she would come to Philadelphia, they could live simply in rented rooms.

But Abigail was determined to stay in Quincy. And health and finances weren't her only reasons. For years she had made on-the-spot decisions about the family, the farm, the house and money matters. During John's long absences she had cared for sick children and servants, her dying father, and John's elderly mother. At this stage in her life, she treasured her independence and having "a closet of her own."

Even though John missed Abigail, his life wasn't all gloom and loneliness. As a boardinghouse bachelor, he didn't have to do any entertaining, which suited him fine. With Thomas studying law in Philadelphia, father and son met often for dinner or just to talk over Thomas's courses. John and Dr. Benjamin Rush, who had met each other at the First Continental Congress, became best of friends. John added up his blessings—"good

*Philadelphia was a thriving city during its ten years
as capital of the United States.*

parents, an excellent wife, and promising children; tolerable health upon
the whole, and competent fortune."

Although John wrote Abigail that he felt "bold and strong," his hands
trembled, and his eyes were painfully sore. He'd recently had a number of
teeth extracted, which changed his appearance and gave him a lisp.

During his second term John left for home as soon as Congress adjourned in early spring, and he didn't return to Philadelphia until Congress
reconvened in late fall. His months-long absences made him unavailable

to George Washington or anyone else who might want to confer with him.

John may have regretted that he wasn't part of the political inner circle, but quiet time in Quincy meant more to him. How he looked forward to working in his fields by day and reading and writing in his library after supper! His greatest joy was to be with Abigail again.

John's election for two terms as vice president had brought him the recognition that he had always sought. But he was still primarily concerned with his own needs. "I want my Wife to hover over and about me," he wrote Abigail from Philadelphia. "I want my Horse, my farm, my long Walks, and more than all, the Bosom of my friend."

As the months passed, John's letters became less self-centered and

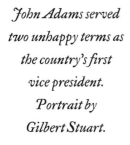

John Adams served two unhappy terms as the country's first vice president. Portrait by Gilbert Stuart.

more affectionate. "I know not what to write you, unless I tell you I love you and long to see you—but this will be no News." Soon he was writing Abigail three letters a week. "I am as impatient to see you as I used to be twenty years ago," he declared ardently. "Three long months before I can see you again. Oh! What to do with myself I know not."

When John had been living abroad, Abigail had pleaded with him for some sign of love and tenderness. Her pleas had been to no avail. John's letters had been short, infrequent and often cool. Some ten years later their roles were reversed. For the first time, Abigail wrote fewer letters than John.

In a sense John had reverted to his lovesick-Lysander days, while Abigail had put her Diana role behind her. "Years subdue the ardour of passions," she wrote. "Friendship and affection . . . will survive."

John did not like that kind of thinking! When Abigail criticized the marriage of an older man and a young woman as a match of the "Frigid and the torrid Zones," sixty-year-old John penned a salty reply: "But how dare you hint or lisp a Word about Sixty Years of Age. If I were near, I would soon convince you that I am not above forty."

If Abigail and John didn't share their thinking on the matter, they at least shared the satisfaction that their "tender twigs" were faring better. In 1794 George Washington appointed twenty-seven-year-old John Quincy to serve as American minister to the Netherlands, the same post that his father had once held. At John Quincy's request, his brother Thomas accompanied him as his secretary.

To their sorrow, Nabby and William Smith's youngest son, Thomas Hollis, had died in 1792. But they were the new parents of a baby girl, Caroline, much to Grandmamma Abigail's delight. Thanks to John's efforts, William was employed at a federal job.

Now that he was in his twenties, Charles appeared to have settled

Twenty-two-year-old Thomas left for Europe in 1794 to serve as John Quincy's secretary.

down. He was practicing law in New York and was engaged to marry William's levelheaded sister, Sally.

In January 1795 John learned that George Washington planned to retire at the end of his second term. By then the one-party system had split into two political parties. George Washington and John Adams were Federalists, the party headed by Washington's secretary of the treasury, Alexander Hamilton. The Federalists were political conservatives who believed in established authority and a strong federal government.

Thomas Jefferson, who had resigned as Washington's secretary of state in 1793 over political differences, would undoubtedly be the liberal Democratic-Republican party's choice for president. The Democratic-Republicans opposed a powerful central government, believing that citizens could find their greatest happiness in a society free of government control.

Having already experienced more than his fair share of criticism as vice president, John began to have second thoughts about running for president in 1796. "I am weary of the game," he admitted to Abigail, "yet I don't know how I could live without it. I don't love slight, neglect, contempt, disgrace, nor insult more than others." John made it clear, however, that if he did run and came in second to Jefferson, he would refuse to serve as his former friend's vice president. Their political thinking was too far apart, or, as John expressed it, in "opposite boxes."

Abigail had mixed emotions, too. John was sixty-one, and she was concerned about his health. And she knew as well as John that if he became president, he would be under constant attack. She described the presidency as "a most unpleasant seat, full of thorns, briars, thistles, murmuring, fault-finding."

Abigail also had misgivings about the part she would have to play. She had made enough sacrifices for the good of her country. Was she expected to make more? Even though her health was a continuing problem, she would have no choice but to live in Philadelphia and perform on the public stage. She and John would be expected to follow in the Washingtons' footsteps and entertain lavishly. And as the president's wife, Abigail would have to hold her tongue. "I must impose a silence upon myself when I long to talk," she confided to John.

Apparently John hadn't always been happy with Abigail's outspoken ways. "A woman *can* be silent when she will," he replied sharply.

In the end, Abigail knew that being president would bring John the honor and fame that had always meant so much to him. That consideration outweighed all else. From Quincy, Abigail wrote to John that the presidency would be a "flattering and Glorious Reward" for his lifetime of service to his country, and she would support him.

An elated John replied that he was overjoyed at her "delicious letter." He couldn't ask for anything more.

Chapter 13

Mr. and Mrs. President

No one was surprised when Federalist John Adams and Democratic-Republican Thomas Jefferson became the presidential candidates in 1796. Neither man campaigned. There were no speeches, appearances or promises.

John spent a glorious summer with Abigail improving his property and building a new barn. "Of all the Summers of my Life, this has been the freest from Care, Anxiety and Vexation," he marveled. That fall he christened their home Peacefield in honor "of the Peace which I assisted in making in 1783 . . . and of the constant Peace and Tranquility which I have enjoyed in this Residence."

When John left Quincy on November 23, 1796, Abigail once again stayed behind. It was just as well. Philadelphia was a hotbed of vicious name-calling. Democratic-Republicans resented the thirty-one tie-breaking votes that Federalist John Adams had cast in the Senate, many of which strengthened the national government. They accused him of being a pro-British monarchist opposed to the will of the people. Alexander Hamilton's ultraconservative Federalists, known as High Federalists, called Democratic-Republican Jefferson a coward, atheist and puppet of the French.

Like John, Alexander Hamilton craved national recognition. But unlike John, Hamilton also craved wealth and power. Aware that he wouldn't be able to control the ethical John Adams, Hamilton worked secretly to have John's choice for vice president, Thomas Pinckney, elected president. From Quincy, Abigail warned John that Hamilton was

An ambitious Alexander Hamilton, who worked behind the scenes to defeat John Adams's bid for the presidency. Portrait by John Trumbull.

as "ambitious as Julius Caesar, a subtle intriguer....I have kept my Eye upon him."

John was crushed to learn that both his good friend Dr. Benjamin Rush and his cousin, Massachusetts governor Samuel Adams, had swung their allegiance over to Jefferson. He hadn't expected Mercy and James Warren to support him, and they didn't. The Adamses and the Warrens hadn't been on speaking terms since 1789. Although political appointments of relatives and friends were commonplace, Vice President John Adams had failed to place either Mercy's husband, James Warren, or her son in a government position.

In December 1796 each state elector cast two votes. Although the ballots were sealed, news was soon out that John had been elected. From the depths of uncertainty and doubt, John's spirits soared. "John Adams never felt more serene in his life," he crowed to Abigail, who was happy for her husband, if not for herself. Nevertheless, she reaffirmed her promise to support him. "I am, my dearest Friend, always willing to be a fellow Laborer with You," she replied.

As president of the Senate, John opened the ballots on February 8, 1797. He had won the presidency by only three votes over his bitter rival, Thomas Jefferson, who now became his vice president. Whether John liked it or not, the Federalist president's and Democratic-Republican vice president's political loyalties were in "opposite boxes."

Inauguration Day was March 4, 1797. Having slept poorly, John was nervous as he dressed in a new pearl gray suit, had his hair powdered and strapped on a ceremonial sword. When he arrived at Philadelphia's Congress Hall in his newly purchased coach, Congress was seated, as was Jefferson, who had already been sworn in. Soon-to-be-retired President George Washington made a dramatic late entrance to rousing applause.

Everyone, it seemed, was there—everyone but Abigail and the Adams

Although John struck a heroic pose as president,
he was disappointed that none of his family attended
his inauguration. Portrait by William Winstanley.

children. "It would have given me great pleasure to have had some of my family present at my inauguration, which was the most affecting and overpowering scene I ever acted in," John wrote home ruefully.

Assuming her usual high moral tone, Abigail wrote John *her* view of the presidency, "My feelings are not those of pride. . . . They are solemnized by a sense of the obligations, the important Trusts and Numerous duties connected with it."

Abigail had recently seen her duty in Quincy and done it. Townspeople objected when she registered in the local school a young servant whom she had taught to read and write. "Because his face is Black, is he to be denied instruction?" she demanded. "Is this Christian principle of doing to others as we would have others do to us?" The boy was enrolled with no more objections.

Back in Philadelphia, John discovered that the presidency was nothing like the vice presidency. First of all, he had the formidable task of following in office the nation's hero-saint, George Washington. And he made the mistake of keeping Washington's Cabinet, unaware that three of his four Cabinet officers, Secretary of State Timothy Pickering, Secretary of War James McHenry and Secretary of the Treasury Oliver Wolcott, were High Federalists who took their marching orders from Alexander Hamilton.

John sent Abigail a call for help. He needed her to spruce up the shabby President's House. More than that, he needed her beside him as his counselor, confidant, defender, sounding board and wife. "I never wanted your Advice and assistance more in my Life," he confessed.

But Abigail was detained in Quincy by the deaths of a young niece and John's mother, whom she had loved dearly. After a more-than-five-year absence from Philadelphia, she finally arrived in May 1797.

But how should the new president's wife be addressed? Because Martha Washington had been called Lady Washington, Lady Adams was a possibility. So was President's Lady, or Madame President. A local wit suggested Mrs. President, while a mean-spirited Democratic-Republican remarked that "Her Majesty" might be appropriate.

As president, John faced worsening relations with the French government. France and Great Britain had been at war since 1793. During Washington's administration the French had seized and plundered American ships in the belief that the United States was shipping goods to Great Britain. After John took office, the French attacks increased.

When the French refused to acknowledge the American ambassador, John announced to a special session of Congress that he would appoint three commissioners to negotiate with the French foreign minister. Facing a possible war with France, he also proposed expansion of the navy and the creation of a provisional army. Special session or not, Congress made only feeble attempts to prepare for war before adjourning in July 1797.

Putting the thorny French situation behind them, John and Abigail headed for Quincy, delighted to escape the capital's heat and yellow fever season. They were also delighted to escape the political heat. Encouraged by Alexander Hamilton, the French-hating High Federalists criticized John for not making adequate military preparations. In contrast, the French-loving Democratic-Republicans, now known as Republicans, called John a warmonger. Stung by every insult leveled at her husband, Abigail wrote her sister that Aunt Cotton Tufts had described her situation as a "splendid misery," adding, "She was not far from the Truth."

Although John stayed home to keep in touch with the capital by daily mail, Abigail spent the summer visiting family and friends. In August, word reached Peacefield that John Quincy had been married in London to Louisa Catherine Johnson, the daughter of a wealthy American businessman and his English wife.

Because John had recently appointed John Quincy to be American minister to Prussia, Republican newspapers accused John of favoritism. Although it may have appeared to be favoritism, John Quincy was well

*During the French crisis, anger between Federalists and Republicans
ran so high that two congressmen came to blows.*

qualified for the post. After his wedding in London, the newspapers
pounced again, calling John Quincy the "American Prince of Wales." One
hostile Republican editor came up with a title for John, too, the Duke of
Braintree.

Anticipating the political turmoil that lay ahead, Abigail was in a
"dark and Gloomy" mood as she and John started back to Philadelphia in
October 1797. And a stopover at Nabby's remote New York farm didn't

help. William had been gone for four months in quest of another get-rich-quick scheme. Although Nabby was without money, she refused her parents' offer to continue on with them to Philadelphia.

As soon as the Adamses arrived in the capital, the round of entertaining began. Abigail held a ladies' drawing room reception every Friday, John received men on Mondays, while guests dined at the President's House for almost every meal.

It didn't concern Abigail that Philadelphia society was conspicuously absent. Her forefathers were the Quincys of Massachusetts, after all! She was the president's wife. She had been presented to French and English royalty. She boasted that her drawing room was the scene of "as much Beauty and elegance as is to be met with in any foreign court."

Over the winter the crisis with France deepened as the French refused to meet with the three commissioners whom John had appointed. And then in March 1798, word reached John that French secret agents had offered the commissioners a bribe. If the United States paid France $250,000, as well as granted the French government a substantial loan, a meeting might be arranged.

When Americans heard about the French demands for a bribe, there was a national outcry. Many Federalists were ready to declare war, while Republicans were furious at John for allowing France's secret offer to be made public. Abigail was worried about her husband. "I really have been alarmed for his Personal safety," she wrote to her sister Mary.

Abigail had once remarked that John's and her "thoughts run in the same channel . . . called the Telegraph of the Mind." It was true. Their viewpoint and thinking were often in lockstep. As a private citizen, though, Abigail tended to advocate more drastic action than John, who had to answer to the public. "I hope we shall have spirit and energy sufficient to arm and defend ourselves, and if that obliges us to declare war, the sooner the better," was Abigail's reaction to France's proposal.

Although John wasn't willing to declare war, he was willing to arm for war. The Department of the Navy was created, which added a secretary of the navy to the Cabinet. The small provisional army, with George Washington as its commander in chief, was enlarged. The Quasi-War, or not-quite-real war, with France had begun in earnest.

A Philadelphia shipyard stepped up production in preparation for war with France.

Behind the scenes Alexander Hamilton arranged to be appointed inspector general, the army's second in command. He anticipated that the French would declare war as soon as they learned about the American military buildup. His next steps would be to become head of the American army, conquer Spanish Louisiana and Florida, and liberate South America from Spain.

In reaction to the Quasi-War with France, and to silence the press, the Federalist Congress passed the Alien and Sedition Acts. "Alien" referred to foreigners living in the United States, while "sedition" referred to any stirring up of rebellion against the government. Three of the acts restricted aliens' basic rights. The fourth act permitted prosecution of writers or newspaper editors who made "false, scandalous, and malicious" statements about federal officials.

Abigail strongly supported the acts. She believed that "most of our troubles in this Country arise from imported foreigners." But John was denounced for signing the unpopular Alien and Sedition Acts into law, even though the law would expire in 1801.

On their way home to Peacefield after Congress adjourned in July 1798, Abigail and John stopped for Nabby to take her back with them for the summer. Abigail had encouraged Nabby to marry William Smith. Now that Nabby's life with William had become so difficult, Abigail tried to support and protect her daughter in every way.

Abigail looked forward to arriving at Peacefield. As a surprise for John, she had arranged to have the kitchen enlarged and a parlor added to the west end of the house. But by the time they arrived in Quincy, Abigail was desperately sick. Doctors and family feared she would die. She lay on what she called her deathbed for eleven weeks with a recurrence of the ague, and what was probably a virus. A worried John endured the "most gloomy summer" of his life.

Because Abigail's recovery was slow, John waited until November before he headed back to Philadelphia. Abigail had earlier remarked that she would be only "a halfway politician" that winter. John felt like a halfway politician himself. After his first day on the road, he wrote his ailing wife: "If I had less Anxiety about your health, I should have more about public affairs."

But the country couldn't afford to have John leave his heart and mind behind in Quincy. With the Quasi-War with France spiraling out of control, a full-time president was needed at the helm.

Chapter 14

The Old Man and the Old Woman

Whether John was worried about Abigail or not, he got right down to business when he arrived in Philadelphia on November 25, 1798. Calling his Cabinet officers together, he asked for advice on the French situation. With instructions from Alexander Hamilton, Secretaries Pickering, McHenry and Wolcott advised John not to change government policy.

John didn't. He told Congress that war would not be declared but the military buildup would continue. The three peace commissioners had been recalled from Paris, and no new commissioners would be named.

The joy had gone out of John's presidency. He was alone in Philadelphia. His "dear Friend" was still sickly. There was no one to confide in who understood his deepest fears and doubts. His eyesight had worsened, and his teeth and gums were painful.

Sixty-three-year-old John felt the familiar walls of depression and lifelong fear of illness and death close in around him. A Republican newspaper editor ridiculed the president and his wife as "The Happy Old Couple," the subject of a 1735 English ballad. And John felt old. "I am old—very Old and never shall be very well—certainly while in this office," he fretted in a gloomy Christmas letter to Abigail.

The state of the nation wasn't much better. The war fever that had gripped the country was fading, and people resented the new taxes that were being raised to pay for the provisional army. The hated Alien and Sedition Acts were condemned as unconstitutional. Protests flared up. Arrests were made. Both Abigail and Vice President Thomas Jefferson expressed concern that Inspector General of the Army Alexander Hamilton might make plans to overthrow the government in a military coup.

By January 1799 John knew that he had to control events rather than allow events to control him. Recent correspondence from abroad suggested that the French might agree to peace talks. On February 18 John took a courageous and risky step. Without consulting Secretary of State Timothy Pickering, the rest of his Cabinet or anyone else, he informed

Charming oil portraits of Abigail and John were painted on glass by a primitive painter, Asa Pope, during John's presidency.

Congress that he was sending a new envoy to Paris to negotiate a peace treaty.

The thunderstruck High Federalists were furious that *their* Federalist President had handed the Republicans exactly what they wanted, the possibility of peace with France. They turned on John with more hostility than the Republicans ever had. High Federalist newspapers blasted him. He was called "vain, jealous, and half frantic." Was he insane?

Abigail was known for her belligerent stand against the French. Many High Federalists believed that if she had been in Philadelphia, she would have talked her husband out of his "arrogant" decision. Word came to Abigail in Quincy that the High Federalists "did not like being taken so by surprise . . . they wished the old Woman had been there; they did not believe it would have taken place."

Actually, Abigail was almost as annoyed as the High Federalists. She, too, had been caught by surprise. It did not, she scolded her husband, "in the least flatter my vanity." Nevertheless, she was in complete agreement with John's decision. She declared that the High Federalists should have known that "the old woman . . . considered the measure a master stroke of policy." From Europe, John Quincy praised his father for acting "not as a man of a party, but as a man of the whole nation."

To make certain that the Senate would confirm his appointment of an envoy, John tightened American peace demands and named two additional envoys. After some debate Congress confirmed the three envoys, then adjourned on March 3, 1799. John left immediately for Peacefield.

With tensions in his own party at fever pitch, John spent the next seven months in Quincy. Critics grumbled that George Washington had never been away from the capital for more than three months. John pointed out that letters reached him from Philadelphia in four days, and he took care of his correspondence daily. Furthermore, he added, his wife was in poor health and needed him. Although Abigail was still frail and thin, she was well enough to call on family and friends. John was the one who needed his wife and her reassuring and comforting presence.

Abigail was in no hurry for John to return, either. "When the President thinks it necessary for him to be at Philadelphia he will go, but not an hour before to please friends or silence foes," she commented tartly.

Away from the capital's explosive atmosphere, John had time to reflect on his future. And his future didn't look bright. Because his appointment of the peace envoys to France had enraged the High Federalists in his own party, John knew they wouldn't support him in the next election. His peace mission had no doubt cost him a second term.

John lost both his appetite and weight. He became irritable and critical of everyone. Much as John needed Abigail, he became impatient with her. Convinced that the pressures of the presidency were killing him, he was certain he wouldn't live another two years.

Reluctant as he was to head back, John finally left Peacefield in October 1799. Because of a yellow fever outbreak in Philadelphia, the capital had been moved temporarily to Trenton, New Jersey.

John stopped to visit Nabby at her farm on his way to New Jersey. To his surprise, he found Charles's wife, Sally, and her two young daughters at the farm, too. Son Charles, whose drinking had escalated out of control, had disappeared, and no one knew where he was. He had also squandered a considerable amount of money that John Quincy had sent him to invest in real estate. Furious, John angrily vowed never to see or get in touch with Charles again.

More bad news awaited John in Trenton. Secretary of State Pickering had held up the peace envoys' leave-taking for months. But John would no longer be bullied by the High Federalists. He ordered the envoys to set sail for Paris within two weeks.

When Alexander Hamilton learned that the envoys were about to leave for France, he urged John to cancel the peace mission. He argued that peace with the French would result in war with France's enemy, Great Britain. John listened politely, then directed the envoys to sail on schedule.

Abigail, who had decided that she felt well enough to spend the winter in the capital, left Quincy soon after John. She, too, stopped at Nabby's farm. With no sign or word from Charles, Sally and her two daughters were still there. A troubled Abigail then met John in Trenton, and together they continued on to Philadelphia, where the yellow fever epidemic had run its course.

Despite her anxiety about Charles, Abigail was pleased to find that John's peace mission had "electrified" the public. It was a good omen. To his parents' delight, son Thomas, who had arrived home after nearly five years abroad, would live with his parents in Philadelphia that winter, along with Nabby and Nabby's daughter, Caroline. With Charles still missing, Sally and the girls returned to New York. Abigail's health was better than it had been in years and for once she enjoyed entertaining, even setting Philadelphia's winter fashion styles.

By spring, John knew that he would have to act, and act soon, if he wanted to win the 1800 election. Sensing that moderate Federalists had rallied behind him, he demanded and received Secretary of War McHenry's resignation. When Secretary of State Pickering refused to resign, John fired him. He allowed Secretary of the Treasury Wolcott to stay on as an economic advisor only. With McHenry and Pickering gone and Wolcott powerless, Alexander Hamilton no longer had a voice in John's Cabinet.

After Congress adjourned in May 1800, John rode south to inspect the new capital on the Potomac River. In the fall, all government offices would move to Washington City. Although work had been going on for ten years, Washington City hardly deserved the title of city. Hogs and cattle roamed streets that weren't much more than bumpy ruts. Only six hundred houses had been built, when nine hundred were needed. John was impressed, however, by the handsome President's House, which was nearly finished.

From Washington City, John continued on to Mount Vernon. George Washington had died in December 1799, and John wanted to pay respects to his widow before returning home.

While John traveled south, Abigail headed back to Quincy, stopping to see Charles, who had returned to his wife and daughters in New York over the winter. Drinking had so sapped his health that he was bedridden and desperately ill. Abigail could never abandon her beloved son as John had. But she couldn't understand how Charles, who had received a "good and virtuous" upbringing and education, both at home and at Harvard, had wasted his life with drink and what she called his "vicious conduct." In despair, she mourned, "All is lost. Ruin and destruction swallowed him up."

Nabby's situation was desperate, too. John had arranged for William to serve in the provisional army, but when John set the peace mission in motion, the army was disbanded. William was again without a job or source of income.

Although Thomas was now a practicing lawyer in Philadelphia, his career wasn't going well. Troubled by his son's lighthearted manner, John criticized Thomas for being frivolous, demanding that he make "a total sacrifice of Pleasures and Amusements."

John Quincy's diplomatic career was everything that Abigail and John could have hoped for. But John Quincy was depressed at his wife's failure to have children after three miscarriages and disappointed that he was serving in Berlin rather than London or Boston.

"Happy Washington! Happy to be childless," John had once said. "My children give me more Pain than all my Enemies."

Abigail had disagreed. "I do not consider George Washington at all a happier man because he has no children," had been her response. "If he has none to give him pain, he has none to give him pleasure."

About the only pleasure John and Abigail experienced that summer was overseeing construction at Peacefield. A new east wing was being built that added a large drawing room downstairs and a study upstairs for John.

Certainly John's official business gave him little pleasure. In France, Napoleon had seized power and overthrown the government to become First Consul. Although peace talks had finally begun, little news reached John from Paris.

A large addition to Peacefield gave the Adams family needed space.

A more immediate problem was the upcoming election. Federalist John Adams and Republican Thomas Jefferson were once again the presidential candidates. In the fall of 1800 while John and Abigail were still in Quincy, Alexander Hamilton published a pamphlet entitled "Concerning the Public Conduct and Behavior of John Adams." He accused John of having "a vanity without bounds . . . an ungovernable temper . . . a disgusting egotism" that made John Adams "unfit for the office of Chief Magistrate."

John had the good sense not to respond. But Hamilton was the head of the Federalist party, and his hostile attack on his Federalist president signaled a final split in the party. The Federalists had everything to lose by their inner-party warfare, while the Republicans had everything to gain.

By mid-October John could no longer postpone leaving for Washington City. Although Abigail would follow shortly, they had no idea how long their stay would be. They would live either four years in the brand-new President's House . . . or only a few months. The December election would tell the tale.

Chapter 15

Washington City

When John arrived in Washington City on November 1, 1800, he was greeted by good news. Secretary of the Treasury Oliver Wolcott, the last of Hamilton's lackeys in his Cabinet, had resigned.

Not such good news was the condition of the President's House. Plaster on the walls was still wet, the main staircase hadn't been built, and a temporary bridge over the littered grounds led to the front door. Despite the chaos, the official full-length portrait of George Washington had already been hung.

That night John became the first president to sleep in what would later be known as the White House. The next day he wrote a letter to Abigail that ended with a moving benediction, "I pray Heaven to bestow the best of blessings on this house and all that shall hereafter inhabit it. May none but wise and honest men ever rule under this roof."

Because of a flare-up of rheumatism, Abigail had postponed leaving Quincy for two weeks. When she finally started out, her journey was even more difficult than she had expected. Her driver got lost between Baltimore and Washington City and had to post a man on the coach roof to chop their way through overhanging branches.

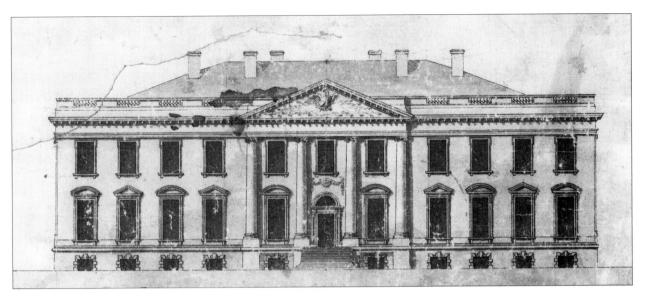

James Hoban submitted the winning plan
for the new President's House.

Once they reached their destination Abigail expressed her usual forthright opinions. "The country around is romantic but wild, a wilderness at present," she wrote to her sister Mary. Nearby Georgetown was worse. "It is the very dirtiest Hole I ever saw . . . a quagmire after every rain," she observed.

At least she was pleased with the view. "The President's House is in a beautiful situation in front of which is the Potomac [River]," she noted. However, it would take thirty servants to run such "a great castle of a House," while she and John could only afford thirteen. Thankfully, the capable John Briesler would be in charge of the staff.

"Not one room or chamber is finished," Abigail continued. The wet plaster made the whole house damp and cold, and no wood had been provided to keep the fires going. And she refused to hang her laundry outside for passersby to gawk at. "We have not the least fence, yard, or other conveniences, without," she complained, "and the great unfinished audience-room [East Room] I make a drying room of, to hang up the clothes in." Despite all the inconveniences, she predicted, "This House is built for ages to come."

With slaves doing most of the manual work, the new capital was as strange to Abigail and John as any foreign city they had ever lived in. Although her father had owned a slave named Phoebe, who was freed at

With no drying yard at the President's House, Abigail supervised hanging the family laundry in the East Room.

the time of his death in 1783, Abigail loathed slavery. It was a peculiar system, she wrote to Uncle Cotton Tufts, that forced "slaves half fed and destitute of clothing . . . to labor, while the owner walked around idle." Unlike John and Abigail, who had worked hard all their lives and were always on time, Washington City's citizens seemed to make idleness and lack of punctuality a way of life.

During the first week of December, electors met in each state to cast their two votes. The results were devastating. The people rejected John's presidency. He lost his bid for a second term. Thomas Jefferson and Aaron Burr tied for president with seventy-three electoral votes each. John came in third with sixty-five. The blow sent him reeling. When he and Abigail could talk rationally about his defeat, they blamed Alexander Hamilton, not only because he had denounced John publicly in his malicious pamphlet, but also because he had split the Federalist party.

Thomas Jefferson understood what John did not. The 1800 election turned on political differences, not personalities. As the country swung away from conservative Federalist policies, the Republican party gained strength, especially among the working classes. The people objected to the high taxes needed to raise an army they didn't want and viewed the Alien and Sedition Acts as a threat to their civil liberties. And the public resented John's absences from the capital for five, six or even seven months at a time.

Tragically, on the same day that the electors met, Abigail and John learned that Charles had died. Although the news was not unexpected, they were brokenhearted.

On her drive from Quincy to Washington City, Abigail had visited Charles in New York. As soon as she had seen her son, whose boyhood charm had lit up their lives, she knew that he was near death. Now she grieved for the "tender remembrance of what he once was." And she ago-

At the time of his death, Charles was thirty years old.

nized over how he had suffered from acute alcoholism and jaundice.

True to the vow he had made the year before, John had not seen Charles on his way through New York as Abigail had. But he was heartsick, too. He recalled those happy days in Europe when his young son had been "the delight of my Eyes and a darling of my heart."

It was a painful time. Charles was gone. The other children were scattered. Abigail and John found themselves living in a great, cold, not yet finished mansion in a strange Southern city. And the people had turned John out of office. Morose and bitter, John talked briefly about staying in politics, perhaps running for governor of Massachusetts or for Congress. Resuming his law practice was another possibility.

By the end of January 1801, John had made up his mind. Charles's death brought home to him how much he had missed of his children's precious growing-up years. Now that he was sixty-four, he never wanted to be separated from his wife and family again. He would retire to Peacefield. "I must be a farmer," he announced.

Despite despair over her husband's defeat, Abigail hadn't lost her sense of humor. "If I did not rise with dignity," she wrote Thomas, "I at least fall with ease, which is the more difficult task." But she'd had to cope with too many emotional blows all at once. "I shall be happier at Quincy," she confided to her sister Mary.

The only uplifting news during those dark days was that a treaty had been signed with France. Although some terms still had to be negotiated, for all intents and purposes the crisis had been settled without all-out war. It was a personal triumph. John boasted with well-deserved pride that he had "steered the vessel . . . into a peaceable and safe port." He considered peace with France the greatest accomplishment of his presidency. And it was.

Angry, hurt and isolated, John spent the month of January in the President's House appointing judges, including a judgeship for his nephew, William Cranch. John had always said that he named to office those who had "merit, virtue & Talents." Certainly his choice of the brilliant John Marshall, who served for thirty-five years as chief justice of the Supreme Court, proved his point. But during his presidency, John had also awarded federal positions to a number of relatives. With Nabby's welfare in mind, he now appointed his son-in-law, William Smith, to a federal post in New York state.

Republican newspapers protested the appointment of the judgeships and falsely accused John of staying up his last night as President naming Federalist friends to office. They labeled the new justices "The Duke of Braintree's Midnight Judges," and the myth persisted. When John

Adams later reviewed his presidency, he stated, "My conscience was clear as a crystal glass."

Abigail had planned to leave Washington City in mid-February to prepare Peacefield for John's arrival in March. But before starting for home, she visited Mount Vernon to bid farewell to a woman whom she had come to love, Martha Washington. Another meaningful farewell was with Thomas Jefferson, who called at the President's House to wish her a "good journey." Their friendship went back many years. Despite their political differences, Abigail and Jefferson admired each other's intellect and spirit.

Jefferson's presidency was still in question. Because he and Aaron Burr had tied, the election was thrown into the House of Representatives. On February 17, 1801, the House of Representatives elected Thomas Jefferson on the thirty-sixth ballot to be the third president of the United States, with Aaron Burr to serve as his vice president.

As the first president to lose the election to a rival political party, Federalist John Adams didn't stay in Washington City to witness Republican Thomas Jefferson's inauguration, as President George Washington had witnessed his.

On March 4, 1801, John left the President's House at four A.M. and started for home. Although the President of the United States wasn't present at the swearing-in of his successor, the peaceful transfer of power from one political party to another after a democratic election was a historic event.

What John's thoughts were on his final journey to Quincy will never be known. But over and beyond his feelings of rejection and self-pity, he must have had reassuring thoughts of his beloved Abigail, who was waiting for him at Peacefield. There they would spend the rest of their lives together.

Chapter 16

Farmers for Life

Over the years John had often dreamed of retiring with Abigail to Peacefield, where they would be contented "Farmers for Life." That dream became a reality after John went down to defeat in the 1800 election. But John was far from content. He was seriously depressed with what his son Thomas called the "Blue Devils." He'd had a say in national affairs for twenty-six years. Now he had a say only in what crop would be planted in which field and where manure should be spread.

With the New England winter still on them, John stayed in the house and brooded. He wrote almost no letters, not even to his children. "If I were to go over my Life again, I would be a Shoemaker rather than an American Statesman," he grumbled. And when he considered the flood of hero-worshipers who had visited George Washington in his retirement, he moaned, "I am buried and forgotten."

Sympathetic to her husband, Abigail covered up for him. She wrote to Thomas that his father "appears to enjoy a tranquility and a freedom from care which he never before experienced." Understanding as she was, she was too busy to fret about what couldn't be changed. There were household chores to oversee, meals to plan, servants to direct, gardens to

Gilbert Stuart painted Abigail's and John's portraits shortly
after John was defeated for a second term as president.

care for and the dairy to run. In a letter to her son-in-law, Abigail described herself as a "dairy-woman," out skimming milk at "five o'clock in the morning."

Still grief stricken over Charles's death, John and Abigail regretted the miles that lay between Quincy and their surviving children. Nabby was in New York, John Quincy in Europe and Thomas in Philadelphia. At least Abigail's niece Louisa and Charles's daughter Susanna lived at Peacefield, which helped to fill the empty house.

Although John and Abigail had a farm to manage and expenses to meet, former presidents received no retirement pay. Fortunately, Abigail had always put money aside and had saved enough to remodel Peacefield and enlarge their property. Her only mistake had been to buy land in Vermont years ago as a "rustic retreat" without consulting John. He'd had no interest in owning Vermont property. "Don't meddle any more with Vermont," he had ordered from Paris.

In the fall of 1801 John's and Abigail's outlook brightened considerably. After seven years in Europe, John Quincy, his wife, Louisa Catherine, and their long-awaited firstborn son, George Washington, arrived back in the United States.

*John Quincy and his wife,
Louisa Catherine, visited
Abigail and John at Peacefield
after serving in Europe
for seven years.
John Quincy's portrait
by John Singleton Copley;
Louisa Catherine's portrait
by Edward Savage.*

Louisa Catherine was sensitive and shy, and she had dreaded meeting her formidable mother-in-law, whom she described as "equal to every occasion in life." Louisa Catherine's fears were well founded. In Abigail's opinion, her daughter-in-law, who had been born to wealth and raised abroad, was a helpless and spoiled young woman. John, on the other hand, found his daughter-in-law delightful. "The old gentleman took a fancy to me, and he was the only one," Louisa Catherine later recalled.

Soon after John Quincy opened a Boston law practice in 1803, the Federalists elected him to the United States Senate. Abigail had plenty of advice. "Keep your mind free from party influence," she directed her son. "Give as your conscience aided by your judgment should dictate." She also had instructions for his wife. Louisa Catherine was to watch over John Quincy's health, diet, clothes, appearance and daily exercise!

For some time Abigail had been urging Thomas to return home. With his Philadelphia law practice still floundering, Thomas reluctantly returned to Quincy in 1803. Two years later he married Nancy Harrod. The young couple lived at Peacefield for five years and then moved into the little farmhouse where John Adams had been born some seventy-five years before.

In retirement, John and Abigail seldom ventured farther than Boston. Instead, their pens traveled for them. Abigail kept in touch with family and friends, while John, after his self-imposed silence, wrote nonstop. In letters to friends, politicians and newspapers, he justified his past political decisions. He even began his autobiography.

An exception to his self-serving letters was his correspondence with an old friend, Dr. Benjamin Rush. When Rush had endorsed Jefferson for president in the 1796 election, John broke off their relationship. Nine years later John made his peace with Rush. "It seems to me that you and I ought not to die without saying goodbye," he wrote. Rush replied in turn, and many warm, humorous and philosophical letters passed between them.

In 1807 John again jumped into the fray. The Adamses' one-time friend Mercy Warren had published a history of the American Revolution. By this time Mercy Warren had abandoned the Federalist party and become a Republican. In her history, she accused Federalist John Adams of losing his principles while abroad and being so ambitious that he

*John and Benjamin Rush's friendship dated
from their first meeting in Philadelphia in 1774.
Portrait by Charles Willson Peale.*

would do anything to gain office. He was also obsessed, she wrote, with "titles, stars, garters, and nobility."

John and Abigail were furious. John immediately responded to Mercy with ten blistering letters. He next sent four articles to the *Boston Patriot* newspaper defending his policies as president. He also gave his version of differences he'd had with other statesmen, especially Benjamin Franklin and Alexander Hamilton.

Every bit as concerned about fame and recognition in his old age as he had been in his youth, John above all wanted to clear his name for the historical record. But the Mercy Warren letters, the *Boston Patriot* articles and his autobiography only revealed John at his self-righteous worst.

As the years passed, many of John's Revolutionary War comrades died. John, however, stayed remarkably well. In his seventies he was toothless, and his eyes had grown weaker. His hands shook from palsy, a condition he called "quiveration," but when the weather was good, he walked four miles a day and rode horseback.

Although Abigail was nine years younger, her health had never been strong. Her chronic rheumatism, which she called the "dismals," sometimes confined her to bed for days. By 1808 she was able to write only in the mornings, with the rheumatism in her hands so painful by afternoon that she couldn't hold a pen. Her every illness became a medical crisis.

In 1809 the Massachusetts Federalist party turned Federalist Senator John Quincy Adams out of office for his Republican leanings. Later that same year President James Madison appointed John Quincy to be American ambassador to Russia.

Now the parents of three sons, John Quincy and Louisa Catherine planned to take their youngest child with them and leave their two older boys behind to live at Peacefield. Abigail and John were happy for their son, but grieved at his living six thousand miles away.

Although Abigail was usually optimistic, she despaired of ever seeing John Quincy again. "At the advanced years both of his Father and Myself, we can have very little expectation of meeting again in this mortal theater," she grieved.

But even at a six-thousand-mile distance, Abigail couldn't resist meddling in her son's life. When John Quincy and Louisa Catherine complained of hardships in Russia, Abigail appealed to President Madison to bring them home. Madison replied that he would send for them if John Quincy requested it, a request John Quincy never made.

Two years later Abigail and John faced a far more serious crisis. Forty-six-year-old Nabby had breast cancer. At Abigail's insistence, Nabby traveled to Quincy in order to undergo surgery in Boston, a radical procedure at the time.

Shortly after the operation, Abigail and John's brother-in-law, Richard Cranch, died. Richard had been John's loyal friend even before the two men courted the Smith sisters back in the 1760s. Only a day after her husband's death, Mary Cranch died. Abigail had always enjoyed a special relationship with her sister, confiding in her on the deepest level. The loss of both Cranches and their worry about Nabby turned John and Abigail's world topsy-turvy.

Nabby remained at Peacefield under her parents' care for a year. Her recovery was slow, and it was a stressful time for Abigail and John. A saving grace during those months was John's renewed friendship with Thomas Jefferson.

Over the years Benjamin Rush had tried his best to heal the breach between the two men—without success. When Jefferson's daughter Polly had died in 1804, Abigail wrote Jefferson a sympathy letter without telling John. The two old friends had kept in touch for five months. But when political differences became an issue, Abigail ended their correspondence.

Acting as a go-between, Benjamin Rush finally brought the two Founding Fathers together. In 1811 Jefferson had retired to Monticello, Nabby was ill, and John was depressed. When a visiting Virginian reported that Jefferson bore him no ill will, John remarked, "I always loved

Jefferson and still love him." Rush repeated John's comment to Jefferson. "This is enough for me," Jefferson responded.

On January 1, 1812, John sent Jefferson wishes for a happy New Year, signing his letter "Friend." Jefferson replied with memories of the years they had been "fellow labourers in the same field." They had much in common. John even humorously pointed out that Jefferson lived at "Monticello, a lofty mountain," while he lived at *Montezillo, a little hill.*"

By this time Federalists John and Abigail had Republican politics in common with Jefferson. For a number of years the British had been seizing American vessels and forcing American seamen to serve in the British navy. Although Republicans were outraged, most Federalists, especially New England Federalists, defended the British.

Both John and Abigail, who had always opposed *any* foreign nation's interference in American affairs, rejected the Federalists' stand. They abandoned the Federalist party and became Republicans, as had their son John Quincy. In 1812, war was declared against Great Britain. John agreed with Abigail when she praised "the Righteousness and justice of the present War with Great Britain."

But even war took a backseat when Nabby's cancer recurred soon after she returned home to her isolated farm in New York State. By spring 1813 Nabby knew that she was near death. Determined to die "in her father's house," she made the painful trip to Quincy. Because Abigail was distraught with grief, John gave their daughter what comfort he could. Nabby died on August 15, 1813.

"The wound which has lacerated my Bosom cannot be healed," Abigail wrote to John Quincy. "The bitter tear will flow long after the Tomb is closed."

During their marriage Abigail and John had lived through great triumphs and painful defeats. But nothing had touched their hearts as did the loss of their Nabby. Only their religion and lifelong faith in God sustained them . . . that and the comfort and solace each was able to give the other.

Chapter 17

Grandmamma and Grandpappa

The months after Nabby's death were a time of reflection for John. Charles and Nabby were gone. The year before, Thomas's infant daughter had died of whooping cough. Two months later John Quincy's year-old daughter died in Russia. John's own death wasn't far off. Life was about family and friends, he concluded, not fame and ambition. He ceased filling page after page with bitter replays of past hurts.

"Nothing is indeed more ridiculous than an old man more than three quarters of a hundred rattling like a boy of fifteen," John admitted to Benjamin Rush. "I am ashamed of it."

Besides, maybe it was time to let the next generation take over. John and Abigail were enormously proud when President James Monroe appointed John Quincy to be a commissioner at peace treaty meetings after the United States defeated Great Britain in the War of 1812. As chief negotiator, John Quincy supervised the signing of the treaty in December 1814.

Despite her grief over Nabby's death, Abigail kept current with national events. "At the age of seventy," she told one of her cousins, "I feel more interest in all that's done beneath the circuit of the sun than some others do at—What shall I say, 35 or 40?"

John and Abigail had more to celebrate in 1814 than their son's success as a diplomat. October twenty-fifth was their fiftieth wedding anniversary. Their thirteen retirement years together had been a steadying influence. They enjoyed a companionable routine, with none of the unhappy lows and blissful highs they had experienced during their years of cruel separations and all-too-brief reunions.

That didn't mean their love wasn't as vital as ever. On the eve of their anniversary, Abigail wrote to her sister Elizabeth that she had been for-

After the United States won the War of 1812, John Quincy (shaking hands, right) was chief negotiator at the meeting that led to the Treaty of Ghent.

tunate to have "gone through a long Life with as few Rubs of a matrimo-nial nature" as anyone could hope for. In some matters, she confessed, she had insisted on her own way, while in others she had backed off si-lently. "Yet after half a century," she concluded, "I can say, my first choice would be the same if I again had youth, and opportunity to make it."

Unlike Abigail, John penned no declarations of love on their golden anniversary. But his closing words in a letter that he had written to Abi-gail before they were married stood the test of fifty years, "I am, and till then, and forever after, will be your Admirer and Friend, and Lover."

Fifty years of marriage didn't mean quiet solitude, however. Children, grandchildren, nieces, nephews, cousins and visitors, as well as Abigail's New-foundland dog, Juno, kept Peacefield hopping. At the center was "The Presi-dent," as Abigail referred to her husband. This was not the same critical father, however, who had been so demanding during his children's early years.

John had found peace within himself. He was a relaxed, playful and affectionate Grandpappa, even allowing his grandchildren to blow soap bubbles with his pipe. He adored Nabby's daughter, who lived with them, describing her as "my tender, my delicate, my lovely Caroline." John Quincy's oldest son was his "friend and companion," while the middle son was his "little jewel."

A Quincy cousin often came to dinner at Peacefield. "Mr. Adams made his contribution to the service of the table in the form of that good-humored, easy banter," he recalled. "With Mrs. Adams there was a shade more formality and her rich silks and laces seemed appropriate to a lady of her dignified position."

If Abigail gave the impression of being formal and aloof, it was under-standable. There were sometimes as many as twenty people living at Peacefield, and Abigail was responsible for all of them. John fussed about his wife's "attachment to every part of her household." But Abigail had little choice. She was the caregiver when there was sickness. She had family finances to keep in order, letters to write, meals to plan, gardens to tend and above all, grandchildren to discipline and instruct. Besides, she explained, "I would rather have too much to do than too little."

Abigail, who had called her children "tender twigs," now thought of her grandchildren as "the young shoots and branches." She had felt duty-bound to instruct her four children concerning their morals, religion, ethics, studies, punctuality, thrift, appearance, penmanship and exercise. She now instructed her grandchildren in the same virtues.

But circumstances changed Abigail in 1816, just as circumstances had earlier changed her husband. Abigail and John were sick for most of the winter. Abigail had such a "dangerous complaint" that she wrote her will. Although spring found them both recovered, they had aged. With humor, John called himself "Mr. Old Folks," while Abigail compared herself to "autumn and the falling leaf."

Many of their family and friends had died—Abigail's dear sister Elizabeth, Uncle Cotton Tufts, their son-in-law William Smith, Dr. Benjamin Rush, Abigail's long-ago flirtatious correspondent James Lovell, and Mercy Warren. At least Abigail and John had made their peace with Mercy Warren before her death.

But the loss of so many loved ones, and her own near-death illness, made Abigail appreciate what was important in life. "This is a very good world," she declared. She patched up old quarrels, became more open to differing political opinions and was less demanding of her grandchildren.

Grandmamma Abigail even scolded John Quincy for being too strict with his oldest son. "A grave sedate Boy, will make a mopish dull old man," she wrote. Perhaps she was recalling her own high-spirited youth, when a neighbor told her that she would grow up to be either "a very bad or a very good woman."

The time that John and Abigail had left was precious, and they enjoyed simple pleasures. Mornings were spent in the parlor overlooking the garden while John dictated letters and Abigail sorted laundry, read or attended to desk work. Afternoons they took "great delight" in riding out. Their carriage followed roads they had traveled for more than fifty years past familiar homes of neighbors whose lives they knew almost as well as their own. They were invited out often. "How frolicsome We are," John quipped. Abigail hadn't lost her sense of humor, either. In a letter to John Quincy, she reported, "Your Father, and I have Lived to an Age to be sought for as Curiosities."

John Quincy had one diplomatic triumph after another. In 1815 he was appointed minister to Great Britain, just as his father had been thirty years before. In 1817 President Monroe called John Quincy home to serve as his secretary of state. Abigail and John, who hadn't seen their son and his family for eight years, were overjoyed. John wrote to John Quincy that the good news had restored Abigail "to her characteristic vivacity, activity, wit, sense and benevolence."

*Mounted troops passed in review as Bostonians celebrated
former president John Adams's birthday.*

Abigail died on October 28, 1818,
with her grieving husband beside her.

The reunion took place in Quincy. What an unforgettable moment! But eight years had taken their toll. John had earlier described himself humorously as "withered, faded, wrinkled, tottering, trembling, stumbling, sighing, groaning." Abigail, who had become thin and frail, remarked that "a small blast would blow me away." Fifty-year-old John Quincy was paunchy and bald. No one cared. They were together once more. During their long separation Abigail and Louisa Catherine had made their peace through a warm and lively correspondence.

Although Abigail had suffered from one illness or another for most of her life, John had always expected that he would die first. After all, he was nine years older. But in the fall of 1818, Abigail fell ill with bilious fever, now known as typhoid fever. For two weeks she seemed to be holding her own, and then her condition worsened.

John buried his dearest friend in the Quincy church graveyard.

On October 20, John wrote to Thomas Jefferson that "the dear Partner of my Life for fifty-four Years as a Wife and for many Years more as a Lover," was slipping away, unable "to speak or be spoken to." With John at her bedside, Abigail Smith Adams died in her seventy-fourth year on October 28, 1818.

Heartbroken but determined, John honored his wife in the only way he knew how. On October 31, 1818, eighty-three-year-old John Adams walked behind his wife's coffin the half mile to the First Parish Church of Quincy for services. There, John's beloved Abigail was buried next to Nabby in the church graveyard.

But not even death could sever the bond between the two old, dearest of friends and lovers. John wrote with assurance, "We shall meet again and know each other in a future State."

EPILOGUE

Although family and friends rallied to comfort John, no one could take Abigail's place or ease his pain. "My house is a Region of sorrow," he mourned eleven months after his wife's death. "Never in my whole life was I more perplexed or distressed than at this moment."

Gradually John began to take an interest in the people and the world around him. His greatest source of pleasure was his grandchildren and great-grandchildren. And his correspondence with Jefferson continued to bring him joy. "I seem to have a Bank at Monticello on which I can draw for a Letter of Friendship and entertainment when I please," he wrote in reply to Jefferson's letter of sympathy.

Although John's health was relatively good, by 1823 his sight and hearing had failed. His mind stayed clear, but he could no longer feed himself and was able to move only with difficulty.

John Quincy's inauguration as president of the United States in 1825 was the crowning event of John's last years. If only he could have shared their son's triumph with Abigail. How proud she would have been . . . and no doubt filled with advice for her "tender twig."

By the summer of 1826 John was so weak that he could hardly swallow. Nevertheless, he responded to a request for a few words to be used during Quincy's July Fourth celebration. "Independence Forever!" was his simple statement.

When John woke on July Fourth, he was aware of the date. But he soon lost consciousness. Near noon he rallied enough to speak. "Thomas

Jefferson survives" were his last words. Unknown to John, Jefferson had died earlier that same day.

About six o'clock in the evening, as the hot July day began to cool, death came to John Adams in his ninety-first year. Incredibly, two of the Founding Fathers who had forged the Declaration of Independence died on that document's fiftieth anniversary.

On July 7, 1826, John Adams was laid to rest in the Quincy church graveyard next to his dear friend and partner of fifty-four years. Mourners who had seen the old couple ride out together in their carriage on fine afternoons must have thought it fitting that John and Abigail Adams were together once more, never to be separated again.

ADAMS FAMILY CHRONOLOGY

October 30, 1735	John Adams born, Braintree, Massachusetts Bay Colony
November 11, 1744	Abigail Smith born, Weymouth, Massachusetts Bay Colony
July 1755	John graduates from Harvard College
October 25, 1764	Abigail Smith and John Adams marry
July 14, 1765	Abigail (Nabby) Adams born
July 11, 1767	John Quincy Adams born
December 28, 1768	Susanna Adams born
February 4, 1770	Susanna Adams dies
May 29, 1770	Charles Adams born
September 15, 1772	Thomas Boylston Adams born
September 5, 1774	John delegate to First Continental Congress
May 10, 1775	John delegate to Second Continental Congress
July 11, 1777	Elizabeth Adams stillborn
February 17, 1778	John and John Quincy sail for Europe
August 3, 1779	John and John Quincy return to the United States
November 15, 1779	John, John Quincy and Charles sail for Europe
January 1782	Charles returns from Europe
March 1782	John appointed first American ambassador to the Netherlands
June 20, 1784	Abigail and Nabby sail for Europe
August 7, 1784	John, Abigail, John Quincy and Nabby reunited in London
February 24, 1785	John Adams appointed first American ambassador to Great Britain
May 12, 1785	John Quincy sails for the United States
June 12, 1786	Nabby Adams and William Smith married in London

June 17, 1788	John and Abigail arrive home
April 12, 1789	John inaugurated vice president of the United States
March 4, 1793	John inaugurated vice president for a second term
August 29, 1795	Charles marries Sally Smith
March 4, 1797	John inaugurated president of the United States
July 26, 1797	John Quincy marries Louisa Catherine Johnson in London
November 30, 1800	Charles dies
December 1800	John defeated for second term as president
May 16, 1805	Thomas marries Nancy Harrod
August 15, 1813	Nabby dies
October 28, 1818	Abigail Smith Adams dies
March 4, 1825	John Quincy inaugurated president of the United States
July 4, 1826	John Adams dies

BIBLIOGRAPHY

Adams, Charles Francis, ed. *Letters of John Adams, Addressed to His Wife*. 2 vols. Boston: Charles C. Little and James Brown, 1841.

Adams, James Truslow. *The Adams Family*. New York: The Literary Guild, 1930.

Akers, Charles W. *Abigail Adams, an American Woman*. Boston: Little, Brown and Co., 1980.

Baker, Raymond, ed. *Boston and the American Revolution*. Washington, D.C.: Division of Publications, National Park Service, 1998.

Butterfield, L. H., et al., eds. *Adams Family Correspondence*. 6 vols. Cambridge, Mass.: The Belknap Press of Harvard University Press, 1963–1973.

——. *Diary and Autobiography of John Adams*. 4 vols. Cambridge, Mass.: The Belknap Press of Harvard University Press, 1961.

Butterfield, L. H., Marc Friedlender, and Mary-Jo Kline, eds. *The Book of Abigail and John: Selected Letters of the Adams Family, 1762–1784*. Cambridge, Mass.: Harvard University Press, 1975.

Cappon, Lester J., ed. *The Adams-Jefferson Letters: The Complete Correspondence between Thomas Jefferson and Abigail and John Adams*. 2 vols. Chapel Hill: University of North Carolina Press, 1988.

Ellis, Joseph J. *Passionate Sage: John Adams and America's Original Intentions*. New York: W. W. Norton & Company, 1993.

Ferling, John. *John Adams: A Life*. New York: Henry Holt and Company, 1996.

Gelles, Edith B. *Portia: The World of Abigail Adams*. Bloomington, Ind.: Indiana University Press, 1992.

Harris, Wilhelmina S. *Adams National Historic Site: A Family's Legacy to America*. Washington, D.C.: U. S. Department of the Interior, National Park Service, 1983.

Levin, Phyllis Lee. *Abigail Adams: A Biography*. New York: St. Martin's Press, 1987.

Mitchell, Stewart, ed. *New Letters of Abigail Adams, 1744–1818*. Boston: Houghton Mifflin Company, 1947.

Nagel, Paul C. *The Adams Women: Abigail and Louisa Adams, Their Sisters and Daughters*. New York: Oxford University Press, 1987.

——. *Descent from Glory: Four Generations of the John Adams Family*. New York: Oxford University Press, 1983.

Oliver, Andrew. *Portraits of John and Abigail Adams*. Cambridge, Mass.: The Belknap Press of Harvard University Press, 1967.

Peabody, James Bishop, ed. *John Adams: A Biography in His Own Words*. 2 vols. New York: Newsweek, Inc., 1973.

Russell, Francis. *Adams: An American Dynasty*. New York: American Heritage Publishing Co., 1976.

Schutz, John A., and Douglass Adair, eds. *The Spur of Fame: Dialogues of John Adams and Benjamin Rush, 1805–1813*. San Marino, Calif.: The Huntington Library, 1966.

Shaw, Peter. *The Character of John Adams*. New York: W. W. Norton & Company, 1976.

Shepherd, Jack. *The Adams Chronicles: Four Generations of Greatness*. Boston: Little, Brown and Co., 1975.

Smith, Page. *John Adams*. 2 vols. Garden City, N.Y.: Doubleday and Co., 1962.

Taylor, Robert J., ed. *Papers of John Adams*. 10 vols. Cambridge, Mass.: The Belknap Press of Harvard University Press, 1977–1996.

Withey, Lynne. *Dearest Friend: A Life of Abigail Adams*. New York: Free Press, 1981.

RELATED WEBSITES

Abigail Adams Historical Society
http://www.abigailadams.org/

Adams National Historical Park (National Park Service)
http://www.nps.gov/adam/

The American President
http://www.americanpresident.org/KoTrain/Courses/JA/JA__Web__Resources.htm

American Presidents: Life Portraits
http://www.americanpresidents.org/presidents/president.asp?PresidentNumber-2

National First Ladies' Library
http://www.firstladies.org/ABIGAIL__ADAMS/FL.HTML

The Papers of John Adams
http://www.yale.edu/lawweb/avalon/presiden/adamspap.htm

ILLUSTRATION CREDITS

The prints and illustrations in this book are from the following sources and are used with permission:

Adams National Historic Site: 11, 44, 58, 73 (both), 78, 82 (both), 94, 108, 118, 119, 120, 121, 132, 133

The Boston Athenaeum: 70

British Museum: 53

Independence National Historic Park: 123

Library of Congress: 4, 14, 19 (both), 21, 22, 25, 30, 31, 32, 33, 37, 38, 40, 41, 45, 57, 64, 86, 87, 99

Maryland Historical Society: 111

Courtesy of the Massachusetts Historical Society: front jacket, 2, 13 (both), 60, 89, 134

Courtesy of the Museum of Fine Arts, Boston. Reproduced with permission. © Museum of Fine Arts, Boston: 24

National Archives: 80

National Library of Medicine: 7

New York Public Library: 69, 97, 114

New York State Historical Association: 71

The Papers of Benjamin Franklin, Yale University Library: 47, 51

JOHN AND ABIGAIL ADAMS

Quincy Historical Society: 103 (both)

Smithsonian Institute: 65

Smithsonian Institute, National Museum of American Art: 129

Smithsonian Institute, National Portrait Gallery: 92

Diplomatic Reception Rooms, United States Department of State: 66

White House Historical Association: 112

INDEX

(Page numbers in *italic* refer to illustrations.)